Thrice As Nice

JC Trez

First ebook/paperback edition 2019

Book design by Passion P.G.M.

Editor: Val Pugh-Love

1

One Hell of a Day

"Mommy, look at me!"

Kenya turned her head in her son's direction and adjusted her sunglasses. She leaned back against the railing of her veranda to absorb the warmth of the sun. Spring was her favorite time of the year, especially since she wasn't bothered by the pollen. Watching Dre play on the swing set his Uncle Kaleb had gotten him for his 5th birthday a few months ago had been their pastime for the last hour. She joined in with his giggles when he jumped from his swing landing onto his feet into the sandbox beside him. Her mind instantly flashed pictures of how terribly wrong that could have gone.

"You're such a big boy, but don't do that again."

This little boy was her one true accomplishment, and she would lay her life on the line to make sure he always kept as much joy as he had at this moment. Kenya's phone rang. She chuckled before answering. Brittany, her head stylist, always called her on Sundays - her only off day - to share some type of drama.

"Hello?"

Brittany's voice boomed through the phone. "Hey, Boss!"

Kenya turned the volume on the phone down. "Hey lady. What's going on?"

Brittany laughed. "Getting ready to leave the shop in a minute. Are you busy?"

Kenya glanced briefly at Dre filling his pail with sand and turned her attention back to Brittany. "I'm chilling. Just enjoying this weather."

Brittany cleared her throat. "Now you know I'm not one to gossip, but guess who I just saw drop Jess off in front of the shop?"

Kenya chuckled knowing Brit would continue anyway, but for good measure, she threw in, "Who girl?"

Brittany lowered her voice as if she wasn't in an empty shop. "Mona."

Kenya massaged her temples and took a deep breath. "Now that girl knows Jess goes through women like underwear. I guess she's a sucker for a broken heart. What I do know is that she better not bring any drama to the shop. Jess's wife doesn't care where she has to clown."

Kenya's phone beeped in her ear and her heart skipped a beat. She frowned when she looked at the unknown number flashing on her screen.

"Britt, let me call you back. My other line is ringing."

Brittany laughed. "Oh, I see. Your wife is calling! I'll just wait until I see you Tuesday. Bye!"

Kenya answered the other line. "Hello?"

"Hey, Kenya."

Kenya looked at the phone again. "Hi. How are you? Who's speaking?"

The line was full of static from interference.

"Please do not hang up. This is not a debt

collector. We are calling you in response to lowering your credit card debt."

Kenya disconnected the call and laughed. "They are getting creative!"

Dre called out to her interrupting her thoughts as he climbed the ladder leading to the slide. "Mama, are we still having lunch with Maddy at 1 o'clock?"

Kenya glanced at her watch and said a silent prayer. This had become their family's Sunday ritual since Dre was born. It was usually a reminder to pull Kai away from work, which she'd become so immersed in now that she'd also opened a second studio. It didn't seem to be working lately since they'd spent the last four Sundays alone.

"Yes, baby. You have thirty more minutes left to play, and then we have to get ready."

Dre jumped up and down in excitement and started to count out loud under the impression that they would leave by the time he made it to thirty. Kenya laughed at his innocence and did a little happy dance when her cell phone rang again. *Finally.* Her wife's voice commanded her attention, and she picked up the phone. Kai had customized her ring tone to the song that she'd sang to Kenya on their wedding day - Jesse Powell's *You.* She giggled from the butterflies she felt in her stomach as she touched Kai's smiling face on her contact picture.

"Hello?"

"Hey, beautiful."

Kenya blushed like it was the first time she'd ever heard her wife say this when, in fact, it was the total opposite.

"Babe, you're going to live a very long time. Dre just asked about you."

Kenya frowned when she heard papers rustling. "Kai, please don't tell me you're still in Houston!"

Kai braced herself for the disappointment she knew she was about to hear in Kenya's voice. "Baby, I'm on my way to the airport… in about three hours."

Kenya pouted. "Not again Kai." She lowered her voice when Dre looked up at her. "Dre is so excited. Why three hours? What's going on this time?"

Kai leaned back in her office chair and ran her fingers through her hair. "I know you're tired of the excuses. I'm sorry baby. I promise I will make this up. I had to call an emergency meeting after a legal issue came up with one of my artist's songs. The album is scheduled to release Friday."

Kenya exhaled. The frustration was evident in her voice. *Why does she keep doing this?* She sighed. "I'll take him to the aquarium this time. Do you think you can make it by dinnertime?"

Kai looked at the picture of her family on the corner of her desk and shook her head in frustration.

"Baby, I'm so sorry. Please don't be mad at me. I promise I'll be home by dinner." She took the phone from her ear to make sure Kenya hadn't disconnected the call. "Baby… say something."

Kenya nervously bit the inside of her lip. "We're important too, Kai. Lately, we've gotten the short end of the stick."

She wanted to be upset but could never stay mad at Kai. She knew the risk associated with opening another studio, but she continued to pout anyway, hoping to drive her point home.

Kai glanced towards the door as Marcus, her engineer, knocked while he entered. She held her finger up, signaling for him to hold his speech, and focused her attention back to the phone. "Baby, I will be there. I will fix this! I promise."

Kenya mumbled. "I hope so. We'll see you tonight."

Kai exhaled loudly. "Kenya, I love - "

Her statement was interrupted by the sound of the call disconnecting. Kai took the phone from her ear and placed it on the receiver.

Marcus chuckled, too familiar with the stress the long hours put on a marriage. "Damn, bruh. I guess the wife isn't taking these long days well?"

Kai shook her head no and massaged her temples. "Marcus, I get it. It's just taking a toll on her with us being apart. My son is getting to the age where he's starting to realize I'm absent, but I'll fix it. What's going on with you?"

Marcus reluctantly took the hint to drop the conversation and suddenly looked very serious. "You're not going to like what I'm about to say, Boss!"

Kai dropped her head and braced herself before mumbling, "Spit it out. This day can't get any worse.

Marcus sighed loudly, and nervously massaged his beard. "I don't know if that's true. You have to see this. Come walk with me."

Kai stood and buttoned her jacket out of habit. Her mind was still on Kenya hanging up on her. *One fire at a time.* She walked ahead of Marcus into the hallway after he held the door open for her, signaling for her to go ahead. They took about ten steps before Kai smelled the faint smell of smoke. *God! Not a literal fire!* She looked at Marcus with confusion on her face. "What the hell is on fire?"

Marcus opened the studio door and Kai shrieked. The studio was covered in smoke and the ceiling dangled above the soundboards as water dripped slowly onto the equipment. Her attention immediately went back to Marcus.

"Are you okay?!"

Marcus nodded his head yes quickly. "This isn't the worst part."

Realization dawned. "What were you working on?"

He cleared his throat and said in a slight whisper, "Blige's album."

Kai turned to face Marcus completely, cupping her head in her hands. "Did we lose everything?" Marcus nodded his head.

Without saying another word, Kai turned quickly on her heels and walked out of the studio. Tears fell from her eyes in frustration. She wiped them away as quickly as they appeared. Marcus followed a few steps behind her awaiting instructions. She walked to the bar in the corner of her office and grabbed two glasses. She dropped a whiskey ball she'd retrieved from the freezer next to her bar in each one. Then, she filled both glasses halfway with cognac and handed Marcus his.

"There's nothing that we can do tonight. I'll start making calls, but there's no need for you to be here. Go home."

Marcus took a huge gulp, searching his mind for something to say. "What time's your flight? Do you need a ride to the airport?"

Kai looked at her watch and spoke her thoughts aloud. "Fuck! I have to figure this out. I can't lose my wife."

She grabbed her cell phone and walked to her balcony as she yelled over her shoulder, "Lock up on your way out. I'll call you tomorrow, Marcus."

He finished up his drink and glanced at Kai once more before making his way out the door. She stood on her balcony and stared down at the busy downtown Houston streets. Then, she hit her favorites and called Kenya's phone for the third time. This time she decided to leave a voicemail.

"Babe, can you please call me back? It's important."

Kai heard the doorbell buzz at her desk and walked back inside. She glanced at the monitor and saw a tall slender man wearing a driver cap. *Damn, I don't even remember calling for a car. What a day this has been.* She hit the button on the intercom.

"Hello?"

She watched the driver adjust his tie and lean in towards the speaker. "I'm here to pick up Kai Johnson."

Kai shut her computer down and pressed the button again. "I'll be right down."

2
Perfect Strangers

Kenya searched her purse for her cell phone, trying to remember the last time she had it. She pressed the phone button on her steering wheel, and it connected. That meant it was in the car.

"Call Amber."

Dre and his cousin Karlton were just a few months apart, and they were inseparable. When Kenya announced they were going to the aquarium, Dre insisted that they pick up Karlton. She needed to call her sister-in-law Amber to make sure it was okay for him to go before heading to their house. Amber picked up the phone on the second ring.

"Hey, Sis! Karlton is packed and waiting for you to pick him up!"

Kenya laughed. "You're playing, but that's actually why I was calling. I'm taking Dre to the aquarium and you know he has to have his right-hand man."

Amber did a mock praise shout. "Thank you! Hallelujah! I keep telling you that you never have to ask; just come get him. If he yells Mama one more time, I'm putting him out! Karl put your shoes on. Your aunt is coming to get you."

Kenya laughed. "Where's my baby?"
Amber laughed back in response. "Girl, in that damn room on that phone. Always. She's into some app where the kids battle each other dancing."

Kenya chuckled. "I'll be there in ten minutes. Ask her if she wants to come, too. I'll see you in a minute."

Kenya ended the call and stuck her hand on the side of the seat, feeling for the phone. After coming up empty, she searched her purse again and opened her car door. She stepped out of the car and something shiny immediately caught her attention. She retrieved her phone from the roof of her car and plopped down into the driver's seat. Dre's giggles forced her to turn around.

"Shannon Deandre Sanchez-Johnson, what is so funny?"

She instantly leaned towards the back seat before he could respond and started a tickle assault on him. Satisfied with herself, she leaned back and handed him a Kleenex to wipe the tears from his face. She ran her fingers through his curly hair and leaned back.

"Your grandma used to cry when she laughed, too!"

Dre's ears perked up. "Grandma DD?" Kenya smiled at him warmly. She never talked about her parents to him, so Kai's parents were the only grandparents he knew.

"No, my mom. You never got to meet her."

Dre picked up on his mom's mood change and was intelligent enough to know not to press further.

"Well, I can't wait to meet her, mommy."

Kenya turned and faced the steering wheel before dabbing at her eyes.

"On the count of three! 1…"

"I won!" Dre squealed.

She glanced in the rear-view mirror smiling as Dre proudly tugged on his seatbelt displaying to his mother that he'd won the race.

"You are the fastest five-year-old in the world!"

Dre nodded in agreement and looked out the window as his mom pulled out the driveway. They sang along to the Lion King soundtrack until they pulled into Amber and Kaleb's driveway. Amber stood to the side with a perplexed look on her face. Kenya opened the door hesitantly.

"What's wrong?"

Amber giggled as she watched Dre sprint from the car to join in on whatever Karlton was chasing.

"That's what I was about to ask you. Was that Hakuna Matata?"

Kenya laughed and stepped out of the car. "That's your sisters' fault. She introduced it to him, and now he won't listen to anything else."

Amber pursed her lips. "So, what's your excuse because you seemed to enjoy it the most?"

They laughed and embraced in a hug. Then, they simultaneously called for the boys to stop running. As they walked towards, the house and the boys whizzed past them, racing for first place. They playfully bickered about who won as they opened the front door to let their moms enter. Amber and Kenya smiled in acknowledgment of their chivalry and said "Thank you" as they stepped through the doorframe.

Kenya called out for Kim who almost toppled her in an embrace.

"Tete, I miss you so much. I never see you or auntie anymore."

Kenya looked at her sadly. "I know…that's why you should come to hang out with us at the aquarium!"

Kim who was now a preteen quickly opted to stay behind. "No. That's okay."

Kenya pleaded with her to come, but she dismissed the idea easily. "Tete that's for babies!"

Karlton immediately objected. "I'm not a baby!"

Kim who was now the same height as Kenya rolled her eyes at Karl and hugged her aunt again. "I do want to come over for a weekend, but not today. I have a dance rehearsal tomorrow."

Kenya pushed Kim's hair out of her face and rested her hand on her shoulder. "Okay, baby. You're welcome anytime. Whatever weekend you decide to come, we'll have a girl's day!"

Kimberly smiled and retreated in the direction of her room. Everyone turned towards the door when the screen door opened, and Kaleb walked in with a huge smile on his face. "Hey everyone!"

Karl jumped into his arms. "Daddy! I missed you so much."

Kaleb effortlessly tossed Karl in the air and planted a kiss on his forehead before putting him down. He leaned into Amber and kissed her cheek before embracing Kenya.

"Hey, sis. Came to get your other child, huh?"

Kenya nodded and smiled as she watched Kaleb repeat the same toss with Dre.

"Hey, buddy!"

Dre giggled and wrapped his arms around Kaleb's neck. "We're going to the aquarium!"

Kaleb glanced at Kenya oddly. "Do you have stock in that place?"

Kenya laughed. "I should." She motioned towards the boys. "Let's go, so we don't miss the show."

Amber stopped her right before she walked out. "You sure you don't want me to pack up the rest of Karlton's things? I feel like we're the babysitter and he's actually your son. We can make this thang official."

Kaleb frowned. "Alright now. You're going too far."

They laughed at him and walked out the door, watching the boys race each other to the car.

~

Kenya and the boys pulled into the parking lot of the aquarium and found a spot near the entrance. She retrieved her sunscreen from her bag.

"Arms out."

She slathered the cream onto their legs and arms before allowing them to exit the car. She stepped out of the car, opened the back door, and waited for both boys to climb out. She grabbed each boy's hand and held on to them until they walked inside the building. The boys' excitement was instant as the aquariums scattered around the entrance grabbed their attention. After she paid for the tickets, they walked towards the back to the whale exhibit. They stopped every few feet so the boys could admire the tanks. When they entered the area for the whale exhibit, they grabbed their almost usual seats on the bleachers. They sat close enough to get splashed but not soaked.

Kenya laughed when the boys immediately joined in dancing alongside the kids surrounding them. The trainer's voice boomed over the speakers and asked who was ready to see the Orca Whales come out. Another trainer had everyone's attention while she worked with seals and dolphins. They were doing tricks at the moment and dancing to the music. The trainers were really entertaining and had the entire crowd participating in the dance routine. Kenya turned around suddenly when a shower of popcorn rained down on her head. The little girl sitting behind her looked down at her innocently.

"I'm so sorry. She is super excited. It's our first time here," the lady with the girl explained.

Kenya smiled and turned her attention towards the voice. She cleared her throat nervously and her face immediately flushed. *Damn, she's gorgeous.*

"No problem at all! Just be glad you're above us, or I'd probably be apologizing to you the entire show."

The gorgeous stranger flashed a perfect smile and winked. "I could think of worse things."

Kenya tried to ignore the way that comment made her blush. She quickly turned her attention back towards the boys. She began to brush the kernels from her lap and hair until she felt another tap on her shoulder. She turned around again forcing a smile.

"Your boys are so handsome. Are they twins?" Kenya smirked and shook her head no. "They're cousins. My son is this one."

She distinguished between the two by rubbing her hand down Dre's back. The stranger extended her hand.

"I'm Taylor, and this is my little sister Lyric. Do you mind if we come down to your bench to avoid that happening again?"

Kenya deliberately shook Taylor's hand with her left hand and made sure her wedding rings were visible. Against her better judgment, she moved closer to the kids, allowing Taylor room to step down. "Sure."

She ignored the heat coming from Taylor's stare as she attempted to make eye contact with Kenya who instead directed her focus on the girl.

"Hi, Lyric. My name is Kenya, and this is Dre and Karl."

Both of the boys waved at Lyric and turned their attention back to the stage. Lyric handed her popcorn to Taylor and moved towards the boys. She immediately joined in with their dance moves.

Taylor laughed. "She never meets a stranger." Kenya chuckled and looked in her direction. She was impressed. "Admirable. I was never that friendly, and I have always been shy."

Taylor feigned shock. "Shy! I would never have figured that."

The announcer saved her from having to respond as he yelled out to the crowd. "Let's make it thunder!"

Everyone started to stomp their feet on the bleachers as the instructor shouted out encouragement for the crowd to get louder and louder. On cue, a huge whale swam out and made its grand entrance with a flip that soaked the entire first three rows. The kids yelled out in excitement. Taylor rubbed the water off her face and laughed. "You chose the perfect seats. I felt the splash, but I didn't get soaked."

Kenya nodded her head in agreement, still avoiding eye contact. "Dre loves this place. If he could convince me to come every day, we probably would." Taylor looked at her watch. "What are your plans after this?"

Kenya also checked the time on her watch absentmindedly. "I'm meeting my wife for dinner." Taylor laughed with disappointment all over her face. "That's too bad."

3

Bad Habits

Kenya approached the hostess with a hopeful smile on her face. She was hoping Kai had already beat them there because she was not prepared for another disappointment.

"Johnson reservation."

The hostess checked her sheet and then grabbed a few menus. "Please follow me."

Kenya grabbed Dre's hand and followed the hostess to a booth in the center of the restaurant.

"This is perfect. Thank you!" As soon as the hostess walked away, Kenya pulled her phone out and checked the time. *Great Kai! No answer, no call, and now you're late.* Their server walked back up to the table, interrupting her thoughts, and placed a basket of chips and salsa on the table.

"Can I go ahead and get your drinks while you look over the menu? Would you like to see our spirit menu?"

Kenya glanced at Dre who was coloring the activity sheet the hostess provided him. "Water for me, fruit punch for him, and a beef nacho for the appetizer - all the fixings."

The server picked up the spirit menu after Kenya never acknowledged it. "No problem. Anything else I can get you right now?"

Kenya shook her head no and pulled out her hand sanitizer. "Dre, may I see your hands please?" He held his hands out over the table and waited for

Kenya. Her cell phone vibrated. So, she squirted a few drops into his hand before reaching for her phone. She checked the caller ID and braced herself.

"Hello?"

She could hear the smile in Kai's voice. "Hey, Baby. What time will you be coming home? I miss you both so much."

Kenya checked her tone to make sure she didn't raise her voice too loudly, and then took a deep breath. "Home? Kai, we're waiting for you at the restaurant."

Kai stuttered. "O-Oh. I forgot baby. I'm sorry where are you at again? I'm a little jet-lagged, and my brain is fried."

Kenya glanced at Dre who was extremely observant to make sure he wasn't seeing the frustration on her face. "The same place we come every Sunday Kai... Tito's."

Kai exhaled. "I'm on my way, babe. I'm just a little out of it. See you soon."

Kenya placed the phone in her purse and touched Dre's hair. "What's on your mind? You're barely coloring."

Dre looked up at his mom with pleading eyes. Kenya braced herself for whatever was about to come out of his mouth.

"Mommy I know that I have two mommies, but did I ever have a dad?"

The question caught Kenya off guard, and she silently cursed Kai again because she was about to have this conversation alone. She knew this day would come; she just didn't think it would be today. "Yes. You had a father, Shannon. He went to visit heaven before you were born. You also have a Dad. Are you forgetting about Papa Patrick?

Dre smiled. He was satisfied with her answer. "I can't wait to see Papa Pat! I miss him."

Kenya made a mental note to have this conversation with Patrick and see when he would be able to come for a visit.

"Chicken or beef?" Dre looked around the restaurant glancing towards the entrance.

"I want to wait for Maddy. I'll get what she's having."

Kenya laughed. "So, you want ground beef?"

Their server walked up with a grin on her face, attempting to join in whatever had Kenya laughing. She placed their drinks, a bowl of lime slices, and the nachos down in front of them.

"Would you like me to go ahead and place your order, or do you want to wait for the third person?"

Kenya glanced towards the entrance and turned her attention back to the menu. "I'll go ahead and order. She always eats the same thing anyway. We'll get the four crispy ground beef taco combo with double rice, and I'll do a green chili enchilada plate."

The server looked up from her pad. "Okay, anything else?"

Kai walked up with a grin on her face. "And two Baja shrimp tacos."

Dre jumped up from his chair into Kai's arms.

"Maddy, I missed you so much!"

Kai hugged him tightly and winked at her wife. "I'll also take a sprite."

She placed Dre back in his chair. Then, she leaned over and kissed Kenya on the forehead. "Hey, baby."

Kenya seemed to release a breath that she hadn't realized she was holding. "It feels like forever since I've seen you. I'm so glad you could make it, babe."

The server returned and placed Kai's sprite and extra napkins on the table. "Your orders will be out in just a moment. Will you need anything else to make your meal enjoyable?"

Kai looked at Kenya for confirmation. She shook her head.

"I think we're good. Thank you."

Kai took a sip of her drink to avoid Kenya's intense stare. Kenya raised her brow and tilted her head slightly. She smirked at Kai obviously trying to avoid eye contact.

"So, this is what you do when you're away?"

Kai looked Kenya in the eyes. She was confused by her statement.

"What? You mean being late? I told you I'm just a little out of it."

Kenya's brow wrinkled. "I'd say. When did you start drinking sodas? A sprite at that, and you ordered shrimp tacos!"

Kai laughed. "Yeah, baby. Being away from you has forced me to pick up some bad habits. I'll get back on track now. I will be spending a lot more time at home."

The server forced her to hold her response when she placed the plates on the table.

"Does everything look good? Let me know if you need anything else."

They nodded their heads and Kai reached for a saucer to give Dre a serving of nachos and a taco. She avoided Kenya's eye contact again. Instead, she picked up her own shrimp taco and took a bite. Dre watched curiously as his mother fiddled with her taco. "Maddy, can I have some?"

Kenya chuckled. "He wants to do everything he sees you-" Before Kenya could finish her statement, she screamed to stop Kai in her tracks before she leaned over to let him take a bite.

"No, baby. You're allergic to shrimp. You can't eat that."

Kai directed her focus to Kenya. "Sorry, baby. I'm not thinking straight. We had a really long night, and I just really need some rest."

Kenya sucked her teeth. "That could have gone really wrong, really fast. Let's just take this to go. Do you need anything else before I call the server over for carryout containers?"

Kai shook her head and rubbed her face. "No, baby. Let's go."

4

Picture Perfect

Natalie crossed her legs and stared into Dawn's face. "I've been here thirty minutes, and we've talked about everything but Friday. I've tried to give you time to come down from your love high, but I'm still waiting for you to tell me about the proposal."

Dawn giggled and flipped her hair. Her cousin Natalie was the only person she knew that was more nosy than herself. She was just trying to make small talk anyway and couldn't wait to tell the world how her man had swept her off her feet. She sighed and smiled as though telling this story again was a chore. "I came home from work and decided to pour myself a glass of wine and watch The Real Housewives of something."

Natalie held a finger up to stop Dawn from continuing. "Girl, no shade. I can't believe that you actually have a job. You're like a different person now. Ryan has been such a good man for you. I've been meaning to tell you that. I'm so proud of you! You're working and going back to school! It also makes so much sense that you'd end up going to law school."

Dawn nodded her head. "I swear he has made me want so much more for myself. Being with him has made me grow up. I am in love. I can't believe I'm actually saying that, but he's my better half."

Natalie matched her smile and leaned in for a hug. "I'm so happy for you, cousin! Now, tell me!"

Dawn leaned back in her chair and smiled as she reminisced about that day. "My doorbell rang. When I opened it, a courier was standing there holding a box. He had a pleasant smile and couldn't hide his eyes roaming over my body. I remember being mildly annoyed that he was standing there so long without saying anything. I asked, 'May I help you! Who are you looking for?' The way I snapped on him brought him out of his thoughts. 'H-Hi... I'm looking for Dawn McArthur.' He shifted his weight nervously, which I thought was funny. I said, 'I'm Dawn. What is this?' The guy shrugged and handed me the box and then asked if I'd sign for it. I placed the box on the ground and signed his clipboard. 'Thank You, Dawn. I'm Terrance.' I rolled my eyes and tossed a quick thank you at him as I closed the door in his face."

Natalie laughed. "Damn, he must have been ugly cause the Dawn I know would have devoured his ass."

Dawn shrugged. "Girl, to be honest, I don't even know what that man looked like. I'm so lifted in love right now that I don't even pay attention to anyone else."

Natalie looked at her in disbelief. "Wow. Continue."

"I open the box that doesn't have anything giving away where it's from or who sent it. This box contains three boxes and a note. I read the note first, of course, because I'm trying to figure out who the hell this is from. It read:

Dear Dawn,

You have a reservation at 6 pm. Please wear the dress and shoes enclosed and bring the blindfold with you. A car will pick you up at 5:30. The timer starts now.

Love,

Ryan

"I pull the black strapless dress and black stilettos out and held it up to me in front of the mirror. It was exactly my style. I raced to the bathroom to get ready because it was already three o'clock, and you know it takes me forever."

Natalie smiled "Pause. Let me see the dress." Dawn took her phone out and handed it to her cousin and then awaited her praises.

"He does have great taste. Girl, you looked amazing, and he looks so handsome, too. Oh, my goodness this is perfect. Keep going!"

"5:25 comes and there's another knock on my door. I open it to a driver in a black tuxedo and a driver's cap. He says, 'Hello, Dawn. Please remember to grab the blindfold.' I think to myself; *my man has already outdone himself, and I don't even know what we're doing yet.* At this point, I can't even contain my smile. I look at the driver who has a blank expression and ask, 'So where are we going?' The driver smiles but doesn't answer my question at all before walking to the car.

"Once we're in the car, the driver instructs me that he is going to play a song, and at the end of the song I should place the blindfold over my eyes. At this point, I'm nervous as hell. I'm in an unfamiliar car with a man that I don't know, and he's asking me to blindfold myself! In hindsight, I assumed the driver was a cop, and I knew Ryan would never put me in harm's way. I was nervous that my man was going through the trouble of making me feel special like this. I've always been spoiled but never romanced. So, the driver turns the radio on and the very first song Ryan and I ever dance to, *A.D.I.D.A.S* by Ro James, starts to play. The song ends, and my heart is beating out of my chest as I place the blindfold over my eyes."

Natalie paused her again. "So, what part of town are you in before the blindfold?"

"Downtown." Dawn continued her story. "So, we drive for what feels like another hour. However, in all actuality, it was about five minutes. The car stops and my nerves are on edge. My door opens, and I hear my man's voice. 'Take my hand baby. I got you. Just a few more steps.' All of a sudden, a calmness washes over me, and I smile. We walk a few steps and he says, 'Step up.' After being led to a bench and sitting, I ask, "Can I take this blindfold off now?' He chuckles and then asks, 'Do you trust me? I nod, and he continues. 'I'll tell you when.' Again, our first dance song starts to play, and whatever we're sitting on starts to move. 'Ryan, what is this? Why are we moving?' I ask. Ryan chuckles again. 'I asked if you trust me, and you said yes.' Before I could protest, he interrupts me by putting a strawberry in my mouth and tells me to bite. Girl, at this point, I was willing to jump off of whatever this was if he told me to."

They laughed together and Dawn continued.

"He continues to feed me fruit for the duration of the song. He kisses my face and lips between bites. Right before a new song starts to play, he tells me that we can remove the blindfold."

Natalie subconsciously moves in closer, hanging on to Dawn's every word.

"When the blindfold is removed, we are in the middle of a lake. There's a gondolier behind us and a picnic lunch of assorted fruit, cheese, potato chips, sandwiches, champagne, and a placard with our names on it. Rose petals are covering the bottom of the boat, and tealight candles are placed along the sides. The sun is starting to set, and the scene is absolutely breathtaking. My eyes well up with tears, and he quickly wipes them away and kisses my lips again.

"He says, 'You deserve all of this baby. My life has never felt as complete as it does with you. That brick brought me to you.' We laugh at the thought of the first night we met, and he grabs the bottle of champagne. 'I'm starving. Let's eat,' he says. I can't take my eyes off him. He has never looked so sexy, and all I want to do is undress him. The gondolier tells us to look up at the front of the boat and smile. That's the first time that I notice the Go-Pro camera in the corner. Ryan fills our flutes and proposes a toast. He says, 'I just wanted to do something special for you. You've been working so hard, and I wanted to let you know that I see you. Tonight is all about you. Here's to a life full of happiness.'

"We toast and take a sip of the champagne. I laugh as Ryan immediately tears into his sandwich. 'Aww, babe you really are hungry.' As I watch him and take in the moment, it's as if the world has stopped. We laugh and talk, enjoying the vibe. We're so immersed in this beautiful moment that we almost forget we're not alone. The gondolier curses under his breath bringing us back to reality. 'I'm sorry guys. I can't just leave this in the lake. I don't know why people won't just throw their trash away instead of in the water.' We nod at him, and I lay my head on Ryan's shoulder after placing a kiss on his cheek. I'm okay with the man fishing all the trash out of the lake if it allows me to stay in the moment. I grab Ryan's face and plant a kiss on his lips.

"The gondolier interrupts us again to tell us that he was successful in getting the trash and how he'd just probably saved a turtle or two. This time, I'm starting to get annoyed slightly. While I applaud his efforts, I just want to make out with my man. I reach over and start to massage his dick under the table. No sooner than I reach for his zipper, the Gondolier calls out to me. 'Ma'am, this is actually for you. I thought it was trash.' I look at Ryan, and he's looking at me with a confused look. I take the bottle from the man and pull the cork to get the message out. I look at Ryan again, and this time he has an adorable smirk on his face. I unroll the paper and start to read it:

Dear Dawn,

*Since the first time we met, I knew there was
something special about you that I'd never
felt before. The love I share for you is
unconditional. No amount of words could
truly explain how I feel about you. My life
has only gotten better over the years that
we've been together. You've inspired me to
be a better person. I know that we were
created for each other, and I only have one
question to ask you...*

"I turn towards Ryan, and before I can say anything, he's on his knee with the ring. 'Dawn, will you make me the happiest man in the world and be my wife?' You know I said yes, girl! And now here we are."

Natalie dabbed at her eyes. "That was the most romantic thing I've ever heard. What's the date? What are your colors? Do you think you need a wedding planner? Does he have a brother?"

Natalie rapidly fired off questions without giving Dawn time to answer any of them. Her heart started to beat so fast that it felt like it was about to thump out of her chest, and her face flushed. She stood and walked into the kitchen leaning onto the counter. The idea of being engaged - even married - was beautiful, but was she really ready to settle down with one person for the rest of her life? She pulled out all the ingredients to start making mini sub-sandwiches. She was overwhelmed by all the things she didn't want to deal with yet. Natalie followed her into the kitchen.

"Can I help? I didn't mean to overwhelm you. Just know that I'm here for you. I love you, cuz."

Dawn handed the jar of jalapeños to Natalie.

"You can open these."

Natalie laughed but never took her eyes off Dawn.

Dawn sighed. "I'm not sure of anything yet, but I'm pretty sure my mother has already started the planning. Why don't you call your aunt and ask her what you can help with?"

They looked at each other and spoke simultaneously. "Nope!"

5
As Long as You're Happy

"Hi, Ken. I'm sorry that it took so long to get back to you. It's um… It's Patrick."

Kenya closed the door to her office and sat down at her desk. She'd just sat her client under the dryer and was excited about this call. It had been six months at least since she talked to Patrick and even longer since she'd seen him.

"Hey, Patty Cake! I know you really didn't think that I didn't know who you were. I was not worried about you returning the call. I know we all have a lot going on. How have you been?"

Kenya listened as Patrick slid his patio door closed and cleared his throat.

"Sorry, Ken. The win- wind is a little high. I've been doing go- good. Yea, I'm actually doing really good."

She raised her brow. Something had Patrick nervous. Shannon always joked about how he could tell when his man was nervous about something because he stuttered. She thought back to the voicemail she'd left him and tried to remember if she had left out any details that she wanted to talk about with him.

"It's been a while since we talked. I know I've had a lot going on. Dre is getting so big, and he's so smart. He definitely makes me believe in nature versus nurture. So many parts of his personality remind me of Shannon. Check your text. I just sent you a video and a picture."

The phone became very silent, and then Kenya heard Patrick sniffle. She chewed on the inside of her lip and waited for him to say something.

"He looks so much like Shannon, and he is getting so tall. I can't wait to see him!"

Kenya was so grateful for the opening that she looked up towards the ceiling and said a silent thank you.

"That's actually one of the main reasons I wanted to talk to you. I really would love you both to spend some time together. I have noticed it before, but it's definitely becoming more frequent that Dre is asking about his father."

Patrick sighed. "Oh! I would love to spend time with him. When are you planning to come for a visit?"

She tapped her pen on her desk. "Well, I'm not sure. I was wondering the same about you. You know Dre's in school until the summer, and Kai just opened another studio. So, it would be a while before we could make a trip. You should come here. You could definitely stay with us."

Patrick smiled. "I'd love that actually. I just need to get some affairs in order, and I'll give you a specific date."

It was Kenya's turn to release her breath. "I was so worried. He's just so inquisitive and observant. He's thick as thieves with his cousin Karlton, Kaleb's son. I think constantly seeing Karlton and Kaleb has him feeling like he's missing something. He's been hinting around about his dad for a minute now, but flat out asked the other night."

Patrick cleared his throat. "Yes, I think it would-"

"Baby, I'm home!"

Kenya heard the phone go silent and chuckled. She'd already known Patrick was dating because of a photo he'd been tagged in on social media. She'd tried to show Dawn, but it had quickly been taken down. They didn't know that he was serious about someone, not to mention living with them. She quickly realized this is what he'd been nervous about. She racked her brain with a way to put him at ease.

"So, that's the boyfriend? What's his name?"

Patrick exhaled and she listened as his shoes clicked from pacing the floor.

"I- I'm sorry, Kenya. I didn't mean for you to find out like this I-."

Kenya interrupted. "Excuse me, Patrick, but you don't ever have to apologize to me for choosing happiness! No one expected you to be single for the rest of your life. Shannon wouldn't want you to be alone. What's his name, and how long have y'all been together?"

She could have sworn that she heard Patrick sigh in relief but instead heard him say, "I'm sorry you had to find out like this. I wanted to tell you first."

"You mean before he made it Facebook official and uploaded the couple pic?"

Patrick gasped and chuckled. "You saw that? It caused such a huge fight that the relationship was almost over before it started. It took him a while to understand that it had nothing to do with me being embarrassed by him but making sure that my family found out from me and not Facebook."

Kenya laughed. "I know one thing. You must have contacted the CEO personally to get it taken down. I blinked, and it was gone. I couldn't even find his name to stalk his page. Did he delete his whole account?"

Patrick laughed again. This time he sounded much more at ease. "No, he didn't delete his account, but we did immediately block both you and Dawn from his page. I know the detective duo you both can be."

Kenya feigned shock. "Patrick!" She laughed, giving up easily. "Okay. You're right. I damn sure tried to show Dawn, and we spent about an hour searching."

Patrick made a humph sound. "Exactly."

Kenya checked the time on her watch. "So, give me details. I have a client under the dryer. We have about ten minutes left to talk - give or take."

Patrick's smile came through the phone. "His name is Damien. He's thirty-four and an architect. I met him at a house flipping seminar, and it has been blissful ever since. He is extremely patient with me, and he's okay with how slow I've been taking this."

Kenya smiled so big that she was sure Patrick could hear her smile through the phone, also. "So, is this serious?"

Patrick smiled. "It is serious. We've discussed marriage, but again, he understands what I've been through. So we are taking it slow."

Kenya heard a knock at the door and glanced at her watch. "Just one minute, I'll be right there. Patrick my time is up. I would love to talk to you again soon. Bring Mr. Damien down with you. You both are welcome. We'd love to meet him."

Patrick laughed. "It's a date. I'll talk to him about it and let you know a date soon. I love you, Ken."

Kenya stood and walked towards the door. "Love you too! Talk to you soon!"

6
Top of The List

"I'm just saying… It's my body, and I give it up when I please. I don't even consider sex until a man has taken me on at least seven dates," Carla, one of the locticians stated.

Several of the women nodded their heads in agreement. Jessica, the only barber, sucked her teeth. "Man, please! Y'all tripping. If a woman tells me that she isn't even considering giving it up until after seven dates, I'm going to show her to the door."

Brittany shook her head. "That's because you're trifling. You treat women like they are toys anyway."

Jess shrugged. "Nah, that isn't true. I'm straight up from the beginning. I don't play games. I let them make their own choices. If you are calculating how much money is going to be spent on you by date seven, you should just name your price as soon as you meet them."

Carla shook her head. "I'm not a sex worker, but you are going to have to put in work for my sex."

Jess tapped her client's shoulder. "Erica, isn't that the same thing? How many dates you willing to take a woman on without any type of intimacy?"

Erica looked at Kenya and shifted in her seat. "As many as it takes."

Jess guffawed. "Aww, man. You tripping. I thought you were going to have my back, but boss lady walks in and you start wimping out. She's married anyway, bruh."

Brittany chimed in again. "Oh, so you actually do honor the sanctity of marriage. You could have fooled me!"

Jess rolled her eyes. "Man, Brittany why you always on my case? You must want some of this juice? My wife and I have an understanding."

Carla chimed in again. "She must not be aware of this little agreement. What was it yesterday when she put a brick through the windshield?"

Jess's face flushed, and for the first time, she was silent. Carla rolled her eyes and looked at Kenya. "You're the only one in here that acts like she's married. How many dates did you go on before you gave it up?"

Kenya cleared her throat and laughed. "Technically none."

Everyone gasped. Jess used that moment to re-enter the conversation. "Exactly! There's no right or wrong way to get chosen."

Kenya quickly interjected. "It wasn't like that. It wasn't on no one-night-stand type stuff. We actually hung out with each other for about thirteen hours before. She invited me out, but it was on the same day."

Erica joined in the convo again. "So, you saw something in her that made you comfortable?" Kenya nodded her head. "We had actually already connected before, sort of. It was definitely something about her."

Carla shook her head. "Well, y'all are definitely the exception, not the norm. Lesbian relationships are totally different anyway. Women are not as bad as men would be getting it on the first night."

Duane, the only male stylist in the salon, waited until his client walked out the door before he spoke. "I couldn't wait until I was done with her. That's my mama's church friend, and I had to be careful not to embarrass my mama. Y'all pick-me women are killing me. It doesn't matter if you slept with a man on the first or one-hundredth night. If his intention is to fuck and leave, he's going to fuck and leave."

Chelsea the quietest, least vocal stylist laughed. "I'm glad someone said it. We are in a new day and age. I will sleep with whoever I want whenever I want. Jess rolled her eyes. "It sounds like sex work to me. Except you'd rather be fired on your day off just to call yourself a full-time employee."

Jess went in for a high five and tried to play it off when Chelsea left her hanging. "Aww, that's cold."

Everyone laughed at Jess. Her face flushed, and she acted as though she was actually swatting at something.

"What's wrong with y'all? Okay, so I have a question. Since most of you are on board with the multiple date rule, what if he doesn't make a lot of money, or at least as much as you do?"

Duane spoke up first this time. "I'm accustomed to a certain lifestyle, and I'm not entertaining a man that can't enhance or at least contribute to maintaining that."

Several women yelled out, "Amen!"

Carla spoke next. "Now, I'm not saying that I'm a gold digger, but I ain't messing with no broke..."

Duane and Brittany finished the lyric for her. Kenya walked past the stylists to the shampoo bowl. "Y'all are a mess. I don't care if they don't make as much money as me, but you do have to bring something to the table."

Jess smacked her lips. "Yeah, okay. How many studios does your wife have now? Twelve?"

Erica finally stopped staring at Kenya and focused her attention on her phone. Kenya laughed. "Two, but I met her before this shop even opened."

It wasn't a necessity that she be wealthy, but her drive is what has made her so successful."

Brittany smiled. "Look at you bragging on bae."

Kenya winked. "I'm just saying. What is the first thing you look for in a mate? How much money they potentially have is not on the top of my list."

Jazzy, the shampoo girl, spoke up. "For me, it's the teeth. It's something about a man with a beautiful mouth."

All the women nodded their heads in agreement. They each shouted out lips, eyes, shoes, and other physical features.

Jess dapped up Erica. "I can't pass by a fat ass!"

Brittany rolled her eyes again. "Ugh, you just get on my nerves."

Jess laughed. "I love you too, and I can't get enough of that fat ass over there."

Brittany blushed and quickly scowled when she realized everyone was staring at her. "Girl, please! Kenya how did you know your wife was the one?"

Kenya's eyes glazed over. "You know, no one has ever asked me that question. It would be the same night that I hung out with her. She showed me her heart."

Jess rolled her eyes playfully. "You're so in love. I knew my wife was alright when she cooked me my first meal. The way to my heart is through my stomach. So, when are you cooking for me, Brittany?"

Brittany sucked her teeth. "I'm not fixing your ass nothing but a humble pie."

7
No Chill

"Dre, I love you. You're going to be a big boy and not give your aunt any trouble. Okay?"

Dre wiggled away trying to get away from his mom's kisses. He didn't want to seem like a baby in front of his cousin. Karlton laughed as Kenya placed a huge kiss on Dre's face. Amber noticed her son taunting Dre. So, she swooped him up and placed kisses all over his face to even the score. "What are you laughing at? You want some mommy kisses too."

Dre smiled and was glad that Karlton was getting the same treatment. He wrapped his arms around his mom's neck.

"I'll be good. I love you, too."

Kenya stood and looked at Amber. "Okay, sis, I'll call you and let you know that we made it. Please call me if you need anything."

Dre and Karlton raced from the room in their typical fashion, yelling the whole way.

Kenya and Amber embraced in a hug. "Girl, you know we will be fine. It was hard the first time I was away from my kids for more than a day, too, but enjoy yourself."

Kenya sighed in relief. "I know he's in great hands. That's just my baby. Speaking of baby, let me get back to this house. You know your sister hates to be late."

Amber's brow wrinkled. "Speaking of Kai, is everything okay with her? I know Kaleb made a comment about not seeing her and that he's called her a couple of times, but the phone calls are short."

Kenya nodded. "Something's wrong. I just can't put my finger on it. I've been thinking she's just exhausted trying to run two locations. This trip should solve all of that and get her back on track."

Amber faked a gag. "Ooh, you nasty!"

Kenya laughed. "Get your mind out the gutter. We're going to Houston so she can make Marcus, one of her engineers, the head of that location. That should free up a lot of her time."

Amber laughed. "Oh, well, that makes sense." They hugged again and Kenya walked to the door while glancing in the direction Dre went. Amber followed her eyes.

"He will be fine! Now, you don't have to go home, but you do have to get the hell out of here."

Kenya laughed. "Okay… okay. I love you and thank you again."

"I love you, too!" Amber shouted through the door slamming.

Kenya stood in shock for a second before Amber quickly opened it back.

"I'm just playing. Go! I will call you every hour on the hour if you want me to."

Kenya realized how ridiculous she was being and shook her head no as she walked to her car.

"Bye. I'll call you if I need you."

Amber laughed. "I hope it's before you cross the state line because I'm not driving to Houston!"

Kenya hopped in her car, glanced at the house once more, and drove off.

~

Kenya unlocked the door and chuckled at Kai singing off-key to an Anita Baker song. "Damn, my baby really is tired. She can't even hold a note."

Kenya walked up and tapped Kai's shoulder, interrupting her jam session.

"Baby, who sings that song?"

Kai looked at Kenya like she had two heads. "Are you crazy? That's Anita Baker!"

Kenya chuckled. "Oh, well I think you should let her sing it!"

Kai frowned and fanned her off. "You're a hater."

Kenya frowned and suddenly turned very serious. "Seriously, babe... Are you feeling okay? Are you getting sick?"

Kai looked at her in confusion. "I'm fine. Ready to get on this road. Let's go, baby!"

Kenya tried to shake the feeling off and made a mental note to grab some Vitamin C and Zinc just in case. "Let's go!"

They placed their bags in the trunk and climbed in the car. Kenya mentally checked off items on her safety list to make sure she didn't forget anything.

"Babe, did you set the alarm?"

Kai shook her head no. "I'm sorry, boo. I thought you did. I'll go set it."

Kenya stopped her before she got out of the car. "Just set it from your phone. Did you forget? Give me the phone. I'll do it."

Before Kai could protest, Kenya grabbed the phone and punched in Kai's passcode. The phone vibrated, alerting her that she'd entered it incorrectly. She quickly punched the code again and received the same warning. Kai reached for the phone.

"I forgot to tell you that I changed the code."

Kenya side-eyed her but decided not to start their mini-cation out with an argument. Kai punched in the code and handed the phone back to Kenya.

"There you go, babe. Set it for me, please."

Kenya set the alarm and the timer on the lights. Then, she made sure to turn the thermostat up to eighty degrees. She placed Kai's phone back in the console and stared out the window. *Why the hell did she change her passcode after all these years?* Kai was aware that Kenya was in her head overthinking. She touched her thigh before speaking.

"It's my birthday, babe. I'm just trying to switch it up a little bit."

Kenya shook her head and attempted to lighten the mood. "It's okay. That's your phone. You can make your passcode whatever you want it to be." She changed the playlist to a mix that she'd just made and turned the volume up slightly. As Jesse Powell crooned out the lyrics to *You*, Kai hit the forward button on the steering wheel and changed the song.

"I hate his voice."

Kenya leaned over and touched her forehead.

"Okay, so you're not feverish. Babe, what the hell is wrong? Since when do you hate that song?"

Kai's brow furrowed. "Since forever."

Kenya sucked her teeth. "So, why did you sing it to me at our wedding?"

Kai laughed. "I said I hate his voice, not the song. I love my voice. That's why I sang it!"

They laughed and talked almost the whole drive. They talked about everything from politics to reality tv. It felt like old times. Kenya smiled and leaned over to kiss Kai's cheek. This trip would be good for them if this was any indication of what was to come. Kai pulled into the parking garage of her building.

"Time flies when you're having fun. We're here!"

Kenya giggled from excitement. This would be the first time that she'd actually been in the new location since the renovations. Marcus greeted them at the door.

"What's up boss? Hey, boss lady."

Kenya smiled and embraced Marcus in a hug.

"I haven't seen you in a while. How's the family? I hope I get to see Veronica while we're here."

Marcus laughed. "You sound just like her. She'll be here in fifteen minutes."

Kai walked into her office. "Has it been slow today?"

Marcus waited until Kenya sat and then he took a seat on the sofa.

"Macon came by earlier and recorded a few tracks, but that's about it. What brings y'all out here though? I was starting to think you didn't love us anymore."

Kai laughed. "Never that. This is my baby, too. I just needed to spend some time with my family."

Marcus nodded his head in agreement. "I understand. I've been holding the fort down though!"

Kai dapped Marcus up. "I really appreciate that, too, which is the main reason that we came out here. You're my right-hand man, and I trust you. I know that you love this place as much as I do, so I am promoting you to GM of the Houston branch."

Marcus stood and looked Kai in the eyes. "Aww, man! Thank you so much!"

She shook his hand and pulled him into a hug. "You deserve it. Like you said, you've been keeping this place afloat while I took care of the home front. Let me hear some of what Macon did."

Marcus stood up and led them towards the studio.

"Honestly, I'm going to say this is some of his best work," he said as they followed closely behind him.

When they walked into the studio, Kenya stared at the ceiling. "What happened here?"

Marcus rubbed his head. "A pipe burst from the floor above us and flooded the ceiling. It was worse than this, but we were back up and running in about three days. The insurance check came, too, from the damage claim for the ceiling. I put it on your desk."

Kai sat in the chair next to Marcus. "Well, Mr. GM, I guess your first order of business is getting this ceiling repaired. I'll add you to all of the accounts before I leave"

Marcus laughed. "That's cold there. I'll get on it. I'm up for the challenge."

Kai nodded. "I already know. That's why you're the perfect choice. Let me hear something."

Marcus advised that the track was already queued up. Kai sat waiting for it to play. Marcus laughed before he leaned over and pressed the button in front of Kai to start the track.

"You're the one sitting at the controls. Don't tell me you've gotten rusty already."

The beat started to boom through the speakers and drowned out Kai's response. They listened to a couple of tracks until the ringing of the doorbell alerted them. Marcus pulled up the camera and buzzed Veronica in before advising of their location. She walked into the studio and instantly embraced Kenya in a hug.

"I've missed you so much, Kenya! It's been so long since I've seen you. I'm so glad you came this time. Where's that handsome little boy?"

Kenya smiled. "He's with his aunt and uncle. I'm so happy to see you, too. I asked about you as soon as I saw Marcus."

Veronica gave Kai a hug and went to stand behind Marcus. "So, what's on the agenda? I know how you two do when you get together with music. Kenya and I don't mind getting out of your hair. I'm hungry and want to go get a Turkey Leg. Have you heard of our turkey leg spot?"

Kai looked at Kenya. "I'm hungry, too. You want to try that, babe?"

Kenya stood. "You know I never turn down food!"

Kai looked at Marcus. "Anything pressing that you need from me, GM? We'll discuss numbers later on."

Veronica looked from Kai to Marcus. "GM? Did you get promoted?"

Marcus smiled proudly. "I did! Kai just turned the Houston Branch over to me."

Veronica wrapped her arms around Marcus's neck. "I'm so proud of you, baby! In that case, I'm getting two turkey legs!"

Everyone laughed and gathered their things to walk out. Veronica paused at the door. "Y'all can ride with me. I'm in the SUV."

They pulled up to the spot, and the line was long. Marcus shook his head.

"Don't be deterred by the line; they move fast. They just opened about thirty minutes ago, so this is the perfect time."

They walked up and grabbed their place in the line. "Kay-Kay! Hey girl! I thought my eyes were playing tricks on me!"

Kenya eyed the curvy woman that was hanging on to her wife and waited for Kai's response. Kai nervously peeled the woman's hands off of her.

"I'm sorry. You must have me mistaken."

The woman stepped back shocked and frowned. "What? Kay-Kay, it's me, Birdie. I know I look different outside of my prison orange but not that different!"

Kai laughed. "I'm sorry. I'm not Kay-Kay. You have me mistaken."

The woman's face immediately flushed from embarrassment. "Ma'am, I'm so sorry! You most definitely have a twin! You look just like my friend Kay-Kay, except she's…um, feminine."

Kai laughed nervously. "It's okay. You just caught me off guard."

She glanced briefly at the frown on Kenya's face. "You are about to have my wife kill me."

Birdie finally paid attention to Kenya and looked her up and down. "Humph too bad about that. You're a cutie."

Kenya frowned and stepped towards Birdie but was immediately blocked by Kai.

"Have a good day, ma'am. You're about to lose your spot."

Birdie frowned and raised her finger, but her reply but was interrupted by her friend yelling for her to come on.

"Yeah ok. You got that."

She turned and walked away with a little extra oomph. Kai kissed Kenya's cheek.

"Calm down, killer. She ain't worth it. Let's not let it ruin the day."

Veronica sucked her teeth. "The only thing ruined was that lazy wig on her head. Ratchet self."

They all laughed and checked out the menu on the easel they were standing by. Kenya scrolled down the list with her finger.

"Ooh, I'm doing the Cajun Crawfish with Mac and Cheese leg!"

Kai exhaled, glad that everything seemed to be back on track. *Man, some people have no chill.*

8
Domestic Disputes

Kenya and Dre stood in the lobby holding the sign Dre made to welcome Patrick and Damien. Kenya smiled at his excitement as he scanned the faces of everyone that stepped on the escalator. She spotted Patrick and turned to face her son.

"I spy with my little eye…"

She didn't get to continue because Dre screamed out, "Papa Pat!"

Patrick stepped off the escalator, squatted, and held his arms out for Dre. "Hey, little man! I missed you!"

Dre ran into his arms and yelped with excitement when Patrick stood up and tossed him in the air. Patrick went in for a hug while still holding Dre.

"Hey, Ken! This is Damien. Damien this is Kenya and my main man, Dre."

Kenya stepped in for a hug. "So nice to finally meet you. I've heard so many good things about you."

Damien laughed, and his deep baritone voice tickled her eardrums. "Likewise!"

His Canadian accent caught her off guard and she smiled. He was not what she expected at all. He was the total opposite of Shannon but somehow seemed perfect for Patrick. He extended his hand to Dre.

"Nice to meet you, Dre. What a cool Black Panther shirt you have on."

Dre giggled and hit him with the Wakanda salute. Damien matched his movements, and just like that, they were cool. Patrick grabbed the sign from Dre.

"This is amazing! Did you do this, or did you pay someone?"

Dre laughed and pointed at himself. "I did it!"

Patrick smiled warmly. "May I have it?"

Dre nodded his head, and Patrick placed him back on his feet before grabbing his suitcase and following Kenya to the exit.

"We're going to stop by the house first, and then we can go to lunch."

Dre looked at Kenya in confusion. "But we have all that food at home that you and Aunt Dawn made."

Kenya looked at Patrick, and they burst into laughter. Patrick shook his head and rubbed Dre's head.

"That was such a Shannon move."

Dre smiled proudly, unaware that he'd just ruined the surprise. Patrick touched Kenya's shoulder. "Don't worry. I'll act surprised, Ken."

They pulled into the driveway, and Kenya released the latch on the trunk.

"Maddy's home!"

Kenya watched Dre run into the house close the door behind himself.

Patrick's brow furrowed. "Maddy?! Is that what he calls Kai?"

Kenya laughed. "It started as a joke, but somehow it stuck. It's a play on mama/daddy."

Damien reached over Kenya and closed the trunk. "That's cute! I wonder what our kids will call us."

Kenya's mouth dropped. "You want to have kids?"

Damien pouted slightly and kissed Patrick's cheek. "I'm trying to convince my fiancé. He keeps going in and out on the decision."

Kenya smiled at their affection. "I'm so happy for you, Pat. You deserve all of this! Are you all ready? Remember, act surprised."

Kenya opened the door and led them towards the family room. As soon as she opened the door, the guest screamed out, "Surprise!!!"

Patrick jumped as if he was startled and Dre burst into laughter.

"We tricked you, Papa!"

Kai's frown caught Kenya's eye, but it quickly disappeared. Kai walked up to Patrick and gave him dap instead of the hug Patrick was reaching for. He awkwardly pulled his arms back and introduced Damien to her. They shook hands and greeted each other. Patrick made his way around the room, embracing everyone and introducing Damien simultaneously. Fifteen of their closest friends had shown up to welcome them home, including the realtor who'd sold his old home. Dawn held on to Patrick and Damien the longest.

"I've missed you so much. I'm so glad you're here. Both of you."

When she finally released them, Patrick grabbed her hand. "What a beautiful ring. My little baby has grown up! I'm so happy for you. Where is the fiancé? I can't wait to meet him."

Dawn smiled proudly and linked her arm with Patrick's. "He had to work the late shift. You'll meet him tomorrow. Now, let's eat! I'm starving!"

Everyone gathered behind Patrick, Damien, and Dawn and prepared to fix a plate. Kenya touched Kai's back.

"Are you okay, babe? That hug was so awkward."

Kai frowned again and whispered through clenched teeth. "When the fuck did Dre drop the Pat and just start calling him papa? Did you know he was doing that?"

Kenya looked at Kai confused. "No, that's my first time ever hearing him do that. It could have just been because he was moving so fast. What's the issue with it if he did just drop Pat and say Papa?"

Kai's voice escalated slightly. "He isn't his fucking Papa!"

Several of the guests turned in their direction, and Dawn and Pat walked up to them. "Is everything okay?"

Kenya faked a smile and excused herself to the restroom. "I need to use the restroom. I'll be right back. Dawn, will you check to see if Dre wants anything to eat?"

Dawn nodded her head in agreement and watched Kenya avoid eye contact with her. As soon as Kenya was out of her sight, she focused her attention on Kai. "Is everything okay? What were you yelling about?"

Kai sucked her teeth and ignored Dawn's question. "Excuse me, Patrick. I don't mean to be a party pooper, but I need to run to the office. Can you tell Kenya I'll be back?"

Kai exited the house quickly, slamming the door on her way out. Dawn and Patrick stared at each other slightly in shock. Dawn placed her plate down. "Will you please fix Dre something? I'm going to check on Kenya."

Dawn walked towards Kenya's bedroom and saw the light coming from underneath the bathroom door. She stood there silently listening to Kenya's sniffles. She tapped on the door lightly and immediately heard rustling and Kenya's shaky voice.

"The guest bathroom is right up the hall."

"Ken, it's me. Open the door."

Dawn stepped back when she heard the door unlock. She stared at Kenya's tear-streaked face. "What's going on with y'all? What was that about?"

Kenya shook her head. "I don't know what's going on with her. Ever since she came back from Houston, she's been so mean and short-tempered. I feel like I'm losing my wife."

Dawn handed Kenya a Kleenex. "What do you think it is? Stress from work or someone else?"

Kenya sighed heavily. "I don't know. It's just been so many little things. Maybe it is someone else, but I wish she'd just tell me."

Dawn massaged her temples. "Little things like what?"

Kenya glanced toward the bedroom door. "I don't want her to overhear me."

Dawn put her hand on her shoulder. "She left. Told us to tell you she'd be back."

Kenya dabbed at the tear in her eye. "Stuff like this. Why did she leave when we're hosting a welcome home party? She changed the lock code on her phone. A few weeks back when we went to Houston, this woman was all over her, but Kai acted like she didn't know who she was and that the woman was mistaken. I convinced myself I was tripping, but I'm not so sure."

Dawn stood. "We'll get to bottom of this. You know I'm always available to help you hide a body!"

Kenya laughed. "Leave it to you to make me laugh."

Dawn embraced her in a hug. "Leave it to me to provide your alibi, too!"

9
Raw Talent

Dre and Damien stood at the batting cage while Patrick adjusted the speed of the machine that would pitch the softball. Damien demonstrated techniques to hold the bat correctly while Dre watched him intently. Dre matched his movements and was excited to be learning something new. Damien stepped back to show that he impressed. "You sure you haven't done this before? You're a natural."

Dre smiled proudly. "This is my first time." Patrick stepped away from the machine and walked towards them.

"Okay. We're ready."

He led Dre to the mound and squatted.

"This is where you will stand. I set the machine to the lowest speed to let you start practicing. It's okay if you don't hit it. Practice makes you better!"

Patrick stood and walked behind the protective cage. Dre corrected his form and swung the bat up the way Damien had shown him. The ball shot out, coming directly towards him. Dre connected with a loud 'clack' sending the ball barreling towards the net. Damien and Pat looked at each other wide-eyed.

"What the hell?!"

Dre continued to hit ball after ball with perfect form. He was so impressive that another man working with a team of little boys stopped and stared. The machine beeped indicating that the speed was about to go up a level. Once again, Dre connected, sending the ball flying into the net. Damien looked at Patrick, whose mouth was wide open.

"So, we have a child prodigy on our hands."

Patrick nodded his head. "I know this is going to sound crazy because I feel crazy saying it. But Shannon was exceptional in baseball. He was on a full-ride scholarship and being scouted before he tore his rotator cuff. A group of boys in the freshman dorm pushed him out the window. Do you think it's possible?"

Damien shook his head in awe. "At this point, I'd say anything is possible. We are staring at something that defies all logic."

The man watching from the other cage approached them. "Hi, gentlemen. He's amazing. Is he your son?"

Damien smiled and pointed at Patrick. Patrick stuttered out, "Yes. He's my God Son."

The man extended his hand. "I'm Coach Ballard. My team is the Raptors. Who does he play for?"

Patrick removed his baseball cap. "He doesn't play for anyone. Would you believe this is his first time ever hitting the ball?"

Coach reached into his back pocket and retrieved his wallet. "How old is he?"

Patrick laughed. "Five."

Coach handed a business card to him. "I'm not telling you to bring him to me, but I'm definitely saying he needs to be in someone's league. That's raw talent!"

The machine beeped again to alert a speed change. Everyone in the vicinity of their cage focused their attention on Dre. He never missed a ball. When the machine beeped to alert that the session was over, the bystanders erupted in applause. Dre stepped off the mound and turned to look at all the people clapping and shouting at him. He ran to Patrick and buried his face in his leg.

"Papa, what did I do? Why are they yelling?"

Patrick removed the hard hat from his head and palmed his curly hair.

"You didn't do anything wrong. They are clapping because they're happy. You made them happy. You should wave at them."

Dre faced the crowd and waved. That was the only invitation the little league team needed as they immediately ran towards him and started to all talk at once.

"I hope you come to play on our team. We're the Raptors, and we have the best coach!"

"How old are you?"

Dre took turns answering each of the boy's questions. Patrick looked at Coach. "I'm definitely going to have a conversation with his mother. I think this would be a great thing for him."

Patrick called out for Dre. "Come on, big guy! It's time to go. I'm pretty sure you'll see them again soon."

They returned the equipment and were given information for three more little league teams before they could make it out the door. Once seated in the rental car, Patrick turned to face Dre.

"Did you have fun?"

Dre nodded his head yes. "I want to do it again!"

Patrick and Damien chuckled. "I'm definitely going to talk to your mom about it."

Patrick glanced in the rear-view mirror. "I have a taste for ice cream! Too bad no one else in the car does."

He pretended to frown and held his head down. Dre screamed out. "I do! I want ice cream!"

Patrick laughed and drove in the direction of the ice cream parlor. "Yes!"

"Wow, this has been an amazing day already. I'm so glad you came with me," he said, squeezing Damien's hand. "I can't wait to have a child with you."

Damien smiled widely. "Yes! Let's go hit some more balls. I like this mood."

Patrick laughed and pulled into a parking spot. "My mind was already made up. You will be a great father."

Damien touched his hand. "We will be great fathers."

They opened their doors and stepped out of the car. Damien opened Dre's door and helped him out.   "I see a lot of my American friends raving about this rolled ice cream. I finally get to be a judge."

They walked into the door and straight to the counter to look at the menu. Dre stared into the bin.

"I want chocolate M&M ice cream."

Patrick laughed. "I guess I'll take the Strawberry cheesecake."

Damien studied the menu. "I think I'll be adventurous and try the PB&J."

The cashier smiled and shook her head. "Strawberry or raspberry?"

"Hmm. Strawberry."

After Patrick put Dre on his shoulders, they watched the ice cream artists prepare their orders. Damien seemed to be even more impressed than Dre. Patrick nudged his shoulder.

"You're so adorable."

Once everyone's order was complete, they grabbed a table outside. Dre dug into his ice cream first and laughed at Damien trying to figure out how to eat it. Patrick shoved his spoon into the bowl and grabbed a spoonful and placed it into his mouth.

"Ooh so good."

Damien laughed and followed suit.

"When in Rome."

He took a spoonful and savored the flavors. "Oh, this is delicious. What an odd combination for ice cream that surprisingly works." They engaged in small talk, mostly listening to Dre explain the solar system to them. A shadow stopped in front of their table causing all three to look in that direction.

"You have some nerve showing your face back in this town!"

Patrick frowned. "Why wouldn't I show my face, Lena? The people that I love live here."

Lena pursed her lips. "You stole the proceeds from the sale of my son's house. You're a homosexual thief! Is this your nasty boyfriend and his child? I bet you were cheating on Shannon with him. Does this child's mother know that y'all are going to turn her son gay?"

The other people sitting around started to stare in their direction. You could hear their whispering conversations as they watched the exchange. Damien's annoyance finally spilled over.

"That's not how homosexuality works, ma'am! It's not contagious! I would appreciate it if you would go on about your business. The only person causing any harm to this child is you!"

Lena rolled her eyes. "All of y'all demons are the same. Nasty abominations!"

She touched Dre's arm. "What's your mother's name, child?"

Dre turned around to face her and stopped her dead in her tracks. "Kenya!" he exclaimed.

Lena stepped back and immediately burst into tears. She looked at Patrick. "What is this?"

Patrick stood and quickly picked Dre up. "I don't know what you mean. Please do not cause any more of a scene. We're leaving."

Lena grabbed his arm. "Why does this child look like Shannon?"

Dre smiled, unaware of exactly what was taking place. "I am Shannon! Shannon Deandre Sanchez-Johnson!"

Lena let out a sob full of hurt and pain and started to hyperventilate. Worry washed over Patrick's face.

"Breathe Lena."

She reached out to touch Dre and fainted. Damien reached out to catch her before she hit the ground. He sat her in the chair and yelled for someone to call 9-1-1. In the hustle of everyone checking on Lena, Patrick, Damien, and Dre snuck off to the car.

10

Yes, to the Dress

Kenya stood at the dressing room door waiting for Dawn to come out.

"Patrick said Damien sat her in the chair and then they ran to the car!"

Dawn laughed from her soul. "That's what her hateful ass gets. I wish I would've been there. Did he say she scared Dre?"

Kenya shook her head as if Dawn could see her. "Girl, you know my baby talks too much. When she asked if he was Shannon's child, Dre told her his whole damn name."

Dawn laughed loudly. "Sweet, lil baby Dre!"

Kenya sighed. "I'm sorry she had to meet him under those circumstances, but it's confirmation on why I've never tried to introduce him to her before. I don't want that influence in his life."

Dawn smoothed her dress down in the front. "I can only imagine the pain she felt seeing a baby Shannon. It's mind-blowing how much that baby looks like him. It's as if you got Shannon pregnant."

Kenya chocked on her champagne. "You're so damn silly."

"Speaking of a negative, this dress is a no."

The lock clicked, and Dawn and the stylist walked out of the dressing room. Kenya gasped and followed them into the fitting area. Dawn's mother started crying.

"I knew it would look beautiful on you!"

Natalie chuckled and Kenya looked at Ms. Ida with confusion. The huge mass of tulle had been her mother's dress pick and made Dawn feel as if she didn't know her daughter at all.

"You are a beautiful bride. This is the one! Don't you agree, ladies?"

Dawn turned around to face the huge mirror. The horror on her face made even the stylist laugh. "Oh, my goodness. It's even worse than I thought!"

Ida frowned. "Well, I think it's perfect. I'm sure you want a hoochie mama dress, but you look so beautiful and regal. This dress has my vote."

Natalie asked for another glass of champagne.

"Whew, Chile. Try my dress on next."

Dawn turned on her heels. "Gladly!"

Kenya laughed and dug into her bag to silence the ringing phone. After seeing the name on the caller ID, she excused herself from the group and walked out of the store. "Hello?"

Lena's screamed from the phone. "Is that child my grandson?"

Kenya took a deep breath, choosing her words carefully. "Hello to you, too, Lena. No, he is not your grandson."

Lena sucked her teeth. "Why does he look so much like Shannon?"

Kenya nervously bit the inside of her lip. She did not want that woman in her child's life. She wished that she'd just drop it.

"I don't know, Lena. If there's nothing that I can help you with, I'm busy at the moment."

Lena hung the phone up in her face. Kenya shook her head and walked back into the store in time to see Dawn walk out wearing Natalie's choice. Dawn did a twirl and giggled.

"Now, this is more like it!"

Ida pursed her lips. "Just like I said, hoochie!"

Kenya admired the form-fitting V-neck dress with lace tulle.

"This dress is cute. Do you love it or like it?" Kenya asked.

Dawn twirled again. "It's in my top three."

Natalie snapped her fingers. "Cause your girl has good style!"

Dawn reached over and took a sip from her champagne flute. "I'll give you that! Okay, next dress."

Dawn continued to try on dress after dress, including Kenya's pick. She settled on a lace, strapless trumpet gown that even got approval from her mother. When she came out in that dress everyone started crying. Her bridesmaids shouted out.

"You're going to make a beautiful bride. That's the one!"

Dawn walked towards the dressing room before stopping to turn around and face the ladies.

"We have about thirty minutes left in the session. Why don't you give your input on the bridesmaids' dresses?"

Dawn disappeared to the back and the ladies voted on the bridesmaids' dresses that the stylist brought out. After settling on their top three choices, everyone started to gather their things to leave. Dawn hugged her mother goodbye and pulled Kenya and Natalie close.

"Let's go get margaritas!"

Kenya yipped. "Good, because I am not ready to go home yet. I have to tell you about this phone call I received anyway. I'll be the designated driver."

Natalie chugged the remainder of her champagne. "Say less!"

They piled into Kenya's car and headed towards their favorite cantina with the infamous dollar margaritas.

"Lena called. She wanted to know if Dre was her grandchild"

Dawn sighed. "I hope you gave her directions to the nearest bridge."

Kenya laughed. "I flat out told her no. Technically he isn't her grandchild. That was not the arrangement I made with Patrick. I don't want her in Dre's life. I hate that she saw him."

Natalie snored lightly in the backseat. Dawn smacked her lips in disbelief.

"Lightweight!"

They pulled into the parking lot of the cantina, and business was booming as usual. Dawn reached into the backseat and shook Natalie.

"Get your ass up, Sleepy Head."

Natalie jumped up like she wasn't sleeping. "What are you talking about! I wasn't sleeping; I was resting my eyes."

Everyone laughed and applied a fresh coat of lipstick. Natalie made sure her boobs were perky.

"Let's go take over the scene! Y'all good? I'm trying to get chose tonight."

They walked in and the hostess told them it would be a forty-five-minute wait. She handed them the buzzer with the flashing lights, and they grabbed a wall. Less than a minute later the hostess called their name.

"Dawn - party of three."

They walked up to the stand shocked that they were passing the people waiting before them. The hostess pointed towards the bar.

"Your other guest already has a table."

They looked at each other in confusion. Dawn grabbed their hands as if to say let's not ask questions.

"Oh, we forgot. Thank you."

They walked towards the bar, and Kenya frowned after realizing who was extending an invitation.

"I met this girl a month ago at the Aquarium."

Taylor stood extending her hand. "Good to see you again, Kenya. I know there's a wait, and I have this table all to myself. I hope you don't mind."

Dawn and Natalie introduced themselves. "We don't mind at all. Thank you!"

Natalie held on to her hand a little longer. "Why are you all alone with your fine ass?"

Taylor laughed and pried her hand loose.

"I always hit this spot on Saturdays. Karaoke night is my favorite."

Taylor signaled for their waitress. "Can I buy a round for the table?"

Dawn nudged Kenya's knee under the table. "So how do you two know each other?"

Kenya poured herself a glass of water. "Her sister poured popcorn on me at the aquarium.

Taylor laughed. "Best mistake she ever made."

Natalie made a humph sound, understanding that Taylor wouldn't be her prize tonight. "I'm going to go sign us up for Karaoke."

Taylor waited until she walked away. "I'm just glad to see you again. I've never seen you here before. Do you come often?"

Kenya's phone vibrating postponed her response. She hit the text button.

Kai: "Aye check this. I'm staying at the office tonight. I guess I'll see you tomorrow."

Kenya powered her phone off and placed her hand on top of Taylor's. "Everything happens for a reason."

11

Broken into Pieces

Kenya put her car in park and turned the ignition off. Kai's truck was parked in the driveway. *Great, why did she have to be home today?* Her entire body tensed up. Everything had been off between them lately, and all they did was argue. Maria, Dre's babysitter's car was gone, so Kai must have sent her home. She took a deep breath and stepped out of the car. As she was unlocking the door, she panicked at the sound of Kai yelling.

"I'm tired of telling you to pick these fucking toys up. Why do I have to step on toys every fucking day? I'm throwing all this shit away since you don't know how to clean up behind yourself."

Kenya dropped her keys on the table. "What is going on? Why are you yelling at him like that?"

Kenya's voice startled Kai, and she gathered all of the papers up from the coffee table. "I'm tired of telling him to pick up his toys."

Kenya grabbed a sobbing Dre and wrapped him in a hug. "It's okay, baby. Calm down. I'll pick the toys up. Go to your room and close the door. I'll be there in just a minute."

She waited until she heard Dre's door close and then she turned to face Kai. "I don't know what the hell you're going through, but don't take your frustrations out on him!"

Kai frowned and spoke as if she hadn't heard a word Kenya had just said. "I've decided that I'm going to go spend a few weeks in Houston."

Kenya paused the movie that was playing loudly on the tv and turned to face Kai.

"So, you're going to act like you didn't just hear what I said. What are you going to Houston for? Business? When did you decide this?"

Kai sighed. "I just need some space."

Kenya chuckled nervously. "Space? From your wife and child? What does that mean for us?"

Kai's brows wrinkled. "I get tired of sitting in this house. We never do anything but work. Where's the fun? All you do is bitch and complain. This is the worst relationship I've ever had."

Kenya's voice elevated quickly. "Damn, Kai! You act like I can't even talk to you anymore! All I asked is how your family would fit into your plans. I'm your wife, not some regular fucking relationship! I should be able to tell you how I feel!"

Kai stood and paced in front of the patio door, avoiding eye contact with Kenya and mumbling to herself before saying the words out loud.

"I just don't understand why every fucking time I want to go somewhere without you, I have to hear your mouth! You have changed, and I don't like it."

Kenya looked at Kai in disbelief. "I changed? No, I'm still the same, and maybe that's the problem. I can't just abandon my responsibilities. If you wanted to do single shit, you should have stayed single."

Kai faced Kenya. Then, she started towards her and stopped in her tracks. She sucked her teeth and mumbled. "It isn't worth it."

Kenya sat. She was caught off guard by her wife's words. "What's not worth it? Me? You about to put your hands on me? Is this where we are now?"

Kai punched the wall and put her fist through it. "Damn you don't know how to shut the fuck up. This is your fucking problem. I don't know how she dealt with your ass."

Kenya's mouth dropped. "You don't know how who dealt with me?"

Kai turned and walked towards the kitchen. "Here you go with some more bullshit. What are you talking about now? Damn!"

Kenya rubbed her fingers through her hair. "You just said you don't know how *she* dealt with me. Who is *she*?"

Kai grabbed a beer from the fridge and popped the top. She took a huge gulp and stared at Kenya.

"Look. I'm not happy. I don't know why I married you except to make you happy. I'm at my breaking point, and I don't want you anymore. It's time that I do what's best for me, and it ain't y'all."

Kenya felt her anger bubbling. She was so hot that she was actually breaking a sweat. "It's time you do what's best for you? When the fuck did you stop? I'm not begging nobody to stay with me."

Kai chuckled. "File for divorce then."

Kenya frowned. "No, you file, since you're the one that's not happy. I'll also make sure to let you be the one to explain this to your son."

Kai shook her head. "That's not my son. That's you and Shannon's son, or should I say Patrick's now?"

Kenya quickly turned her back to hide the pain Kai's words caused her. "I just want to make sure I have all of this correct. You're not happy. After five years, you've realized you only married me to make me happy, and our son is not yours?"

Kai nodded her head as if Kenya could see her. "Correct."

12

Lady in Red

Dawn and Natalie walked into the club and headed straight to the bar. The DJ had the club jumping and played nothing but songs that got the ladies moving. Money showers rained down all over the women dancing on the poles scattered around the room. The bartender walked up eyeing Natalie. "What can I get you, ladies?"

Dawn looked at Natalie and screamed over the music. "What do you want?"

Natalie swayed to the music, ignoring the bartender's sleazy eyes. "Hennessy! I don't want to mix them."

Dawn laughed and ordered two Hennessy and cokes. They'd already pre-gamed and didn't want the troubles that mixing their alcohol would bring. The bartender stepped away to make their drinks, and they turned their attention back to the people in the club. Dawn noticed a sexy, fair-skinned woman in a tight red dress twerking in front of them. Her big, dark, curly hair was a major contrast to her light complexion. If the way she was dressed wasn't enough, the way she moved forced you to pay attention. She was surrounded by men and women trying to get her to notice them, but she'd already spotted Dawn. She danced in front of them and moved through the crowd until she was standing beside Dawn at the bar. The bartender came back with their drinks.

"Fifteen dollars."

The woman leaned in towards Dawn and asked, "What are y'all drinking?"

Dawn eyed her seductively. "Hennessy, of course."

She watched as the woman extended her arm, holding money between her long acrylic nails. She handed two twenty-dollar bills to the bartender and asked her to bring one more. Dawn touched her arm.

"Thank you." The woman placed her hand on the small of her back, sending chills through her body. Dawn stared at her and smiled.

"Don't mention it. I'm Mikayla. What's your name?"

Dawn took a sip of her drink. "I'm Dawn, and this is Natalie."

Mikayla looked around Dawn. "Is Natalie your imaginary friend?"

Dawn frowned. "What? No, this is my cousin." She turned to the empty space where Natalie had been standing. Mikayla laughed, pointing in the direction Natalie had gone. Dawn laughed when she saw she was currently dancing with some guy.

"Oh, you got jokes?"

Mikayla started moving to the music and put one arm around Dawn's waist.

"Damn that's a huge rock on your finger. She must be hella confident to let you out of her sight." Mikayla asked fishing for a clue of her sexuality.

Dawn matched her movements. "My fiancé is extremely confident. He knows he can trust me."

Mikayla finished her cup and placed it on the bar. "Are you going to babysit your drink or come to the floor and dance with me?"

Dawn finished her drink and allowed Mikayla to lead her to the dance floor. They danced with each other until the DJ called out, "Last call for alcohol." Mikayla who was finally ready to leave the floor, touched Dawn's hand. "You want another drink?"

Dawn shook her head. "I need to drive home. I don't know how drunk my cousin is."

Mikayla nodded. "Let's ask her?"

Dawn felt a tap on her shoulder and turned to face Natalie. She eyed Natalie who was swaying to the DJ making announcements. "You look like you feel good."

Natalie's eyes were low, and it was obvious that her buzz was high. "I feel amazing. I ran into my old boyfriend Nate, and I'm going home with him tonight."

Dawn laughed. "Are you going to regret this tomorrow when you sober up?"

Natalie laughed. "No. This is preserving my body count."

Mikayla laughed this time. "How? If you don't mind me asking."

Natalie rolled her eyes and turned her attention to Mikayla. "Who the hell are you? Why are you all up in our conversation?"

Mikayla stepped back and threw her hands in the air. "My bad, lady."

Dawn touched her cousin's shoulder. "This is Mikayla. Mikayla this is my cousin Natalie that I was trying to introduce you to earlier."

Natalie instantly looked apologetic and stuck her hand out. "Sorry about that girl. I thought you were just a random person eavesdropping."

Mikayla shook her hand. "Don't worry about it. I understand. People are weird."

Natalie finished her drink and placed her cup on the table beside them. "It saves my body count because I've already fucked him before. The dick is good, so I'm not taking a gamble."

Dawn laughed. "Weirdly enough, it makes sense. Well, I'm going to head out. Be safe, and don't hesitate to call me if you need me."

Natalie embraced her in a hug. "Girl, I'll be fine. I'll call you tomorrow. Text me and let me know you made it home."

Nate walked up. "You ready to head out baby?"

Dawn checked him out and had to admit he was handsome. He had the height and build of Odell Beckham, Jr., and the face of Idris Elba. Natalie introduced him to everyone and waved goodbye.

"Don't forget to text me. Love you, cuz."

Dawn watched them walked towards the exit just as the lights came on in the club. Mikayla stared at her intently.

"Damn, I didn't think you'd get finer when the lights came on."

Dawn blushed. "Likewise."

Mikayla grabbed her hand. "Come on. I'll walk you to your car."

Dawn followed behind her and actually enjoyed the view from the back. *Damn, she's so sexy.*

Once they made their way out the club, Dawn became the navigator. They laughed and talked as they walked through the parking lot. As they ignored the whistles and catcalls, Dawn hit her locks.

"Where's your car? I'll drive you to it."

Mikayla pulled out her phone. "I'm calling Lyft. I didn't drive because I didn't know how much I was going to drink tonight."

Dawn smiled. "Beautiful and smart."

Mikayla backed her up against the car and placed her hands on each side of her. "Do you have a curfew? Will your man get mad if you don't come home for another hour?"

Dawn laughed. "Why wouldn't I be home for another hour?

Mikayla smiled. "Because I want to eat."

Dawn's face flushed. "Eat what?"

Mikayla licked her red lips and looked at her phone. "Well, it's 2:30. So, breakfast."

Dawn exhaled. "Oh, of course"

Mikayla laughed and winked. "My treat."

13
You've Been Served

Kenya grabbed her keys and called for Dre to come so he wouldn't be late for school. As soon as she was about to open the door, her doorbell rang. She opened the door to a flower delivery man. *I knew Kai would realize the mistake she made.* The man looked down at the clipboard as if he was searching for her name.

"Kenya Sanchez-Johnson?"

Kenya smiled. "Yes, I'm Kenya."'

The delivery man handed her a bouquet of red roses and an envelope. "You've been served."

Kenya dropped her bag in shock. "What the hell!"

Dre walked up beside her. "I'll get it, mommy. Maddy sent you roses? When is she coming home from work?"

Kenya laid the roses on the table in the foyer and grabbed her bag from Dre. She stuffed the envelope in her purse, and then they walked out the door. She tried her best to ignore the sadness in his eyes. It was much easier to lie to him than to tell him that his mother had walked out on them. Kenya decided that she'd wait until she dropped Dre off before she checked to see what she'd been served because her stomach was in knots. *Was Kai actually going through with the divorce?* She pulled herself out of her thoughts just as she pulled up to the drop off at Dre's school. She was driving on autopilot and said a quick thank you to God for getting them there safely. She turned to face Dre in the backseat. "

"What kind of day are we having today?" Dre unfastened his seatbelt and waited until the traffic monitor opened the door.

"This is going to be an amazing day."

Kenya leaned in for a kiss. "I love you."

Dre threw an, "I love you, too" over his shoulder and climbed out the car.

Kenya laughed. "My baby is officially growing up."

She was tempted to pull over into the school's parking lot to read the papers but knew she needed to get to the shop. She glanced at her clock and pulled out into traffic. She had a little under thirty minutes before her first client was scheduled. Kenya walked into the shop and turned off the alarm, which turned on the lights. She turned the satellite radio to a 90's R&B station and walked to her office to drop her things off. She sat in her plush office chair and inhaled. Her heart was beating so fast that she felt faint. *Okay, Kenya, stop stalling. Get it over with.* She grabbed the envelope from her purse and stared at it. Her heartfelt like it was about to beat out of her chest. She grabbed the letter opener and ripped the envelope. She pulled the subpoena out and read the top out loud.

"Lena Duncan vs Kenya Sanchez-Johnson in the paternity of Shannon Deandre Sanchez-Johnson. I can't believe this bitch!"

Her eyes filled with tears, and she yelled out to the empty room. "Is this possible? Can she force a DNA test on me?"

Kenya took her cell phone out and quickly dialed Dawn's number. *Come on, D! Pick up the phone!* The phone rang until the voicemail answered.

"Dawn, please call me back as soon as you get this. It's super important."

She went to her favorites and, against her better judgment, pressed Kai's contact. The phone rang three times and just as she was about to end the call, Kai picked up.

"Hello!"

Kenya held the phone for a second. It had been a week since she'd seen Kai or even heard her voice. The emotions that flooded over her were uncontrollable. Kai shouted again with irritation evident in her voice.

"Hello! Why are you playing on my phone?"

Kenya gathered her composure. "I don't mean to bother you, but I just need someone to talk to.

Kai exhaled. "What's up?"

Kenya read over the top of the subpoena again. "Lena had me served for paternity and joint custody."

The phone went silent for a second but felt like hours before Kai responded. "Who's Lena?"

Kenya took the phone from her ear and looked at it before answering. "Shannon's mother."

Kai sighed loudly. "Oh. What are you going to do?"

A tear fell from Kenya's right eye. "What are *we* going to do? Can you reach out to your lawyer since he's already on retainer?"

Kai laughed. "Nah, that's my lawyer. Did you reach out to your baby daddy?"

Kenya screamed in the phone. "I called to speak to my wife! The person who planned to have this baby with me. Why are you being so cold?"

Kenya gasped when she heard Kai say, "With your sexy ass!"

Anger consumed her. She reached her boiling point when she heard a woman ask if Kai was going to get in the shower with her.

"Kai, who the fuck is that? Where are you!? Are you still in Houston?"

Kai exhaled loudly again. "What I'm doing isn't any of your business. Kenya, what's up? I thought you had something to talk to me about."

Kenya knew it was time to get off the call before it escalated any further. "Yeah, I thought I did, too. Sorry for bothering you. You stupid, cheating bi-"

Kenya didn't get to complete her sentence before Kai hung up on her. She broke down in tears and sobbed loudly. Laying her head on her desk, she screamed her pain out. *"Why is my life in shambles? Why am I being hit with everything at once!?"*

Her phone rang and startled her. She looked at the number that was not programmed, cleared her throat, and answered. "Hello?"

"Hi, Kenya. It's Taylor. Is this a bad time?"

Kenya looked at the clock on the wall. "Who is this?"

Taylor laughed. "Taylor from the aquarium. I was hoping you weren't so drunk that you weren't going to remember that you gave me your number. Did I catch you at a bad time? I was just calling to see if y'all were coming out for karaoke again tonight?"

Kenya stood and looked at her reflection in the mirror. She wiped her tears and applied a coat of lipstick. "Actually, you have perfect timing. A night out is exactly what I need. I'll call you as soon as I clear my schedule of clients."

14

I Want Candy

Mikayla stood at the gas pump waiting for it to click.

"Damn, this car is a gas guzzler. I thought I chose an economy rental."

A black Maserati bumping UGK pulled up to the pump beside her and her attention. She bent down and looked at herself in the side mirror. She laughed after checking herself out.

"Girl, please. You know you're fine!"

She adjusted her skirt and smiled at the handsome man with the smooth dark skin, bald head, and pearly whites. *Ooh shit. Tall and chocolate, and obviously has some kind of bag.* The pump clicked, alerting her that the car was finally full. She replaced the nozzle and leaned over in the car to retrieve her bag. She needed a reason to catch his attention, so she walked towards the store to get a pack of gum. Her long curly hair blew in the wind and her fat ass jiggled as her heels clicked the pavement. She grabbed a pack of gum and placed it on the counter. Then, she glanced outside to see if she'd been watched. Her wish came true as she noticed the handsome stranger looking in her direction.

After retrieving her purchase, she walked slowly back to her car and let him take in all her curves. She got to her car and hit the unlock button. As she opened the door, before she could sit, she felt a strong grip on her arm.

"Excuse me, Ms. Lady." *Got him!* She turned and flashed a seductive smile.

"Excuse me, Mr. Man."

He laughed and extended his hand. "I'm Terrance. How are you today?"

Mikayla put her hand on his chest instead and played with his gold chain. "I'm lucky."

He smiled. "Oh, is that right? Why don't you come ride with me, Lucky?"

She closed the door to the rental and hit the lock button before walking around to the passenger side of his car.

"Where are we going?"

Terrance never answered her. He simply unlocked the door for her to get into the passenger seat. Once she was seated in the car, she took the blunt from the ashtray and struck the lighter to it. Terrance laughed.

"I don't know if you're ready for that, Lil Momma!"

Mikayla looked at him and licked her lips. "I'm ready for everything."

She put the blunt to her lips and inhaled deeply. Her head exploded. She handed the blunt to him and laid her head back against the headrest as she enjoyed the high.

"Damn, that's some real loud!"

Terrance inhaled. "Nah, that's primo."

She looked at him shocked. "Primo? What's that?"

He rubbed his goatee. "It's a high grade of weed."

She looked at him, playing dumb. She definitely knew that a primo was laced marijuana. He put the blunt out and popped the console. He took out a tiny clear jar and tapped it on the skin between his thumb and pointer finger. Then, he put it to his nose and sniffed. She watched him and waited for him to say something. He looked at her and smiled.

"You want some candy?" She nodded her head and ran her tongue over her red lips. He reached down and unzipped his pants.

"What are you going to do for me?" She grabbed his dick and kissed the tip. He moaned and grabbed a handful of her hair. She took her tongue and ran it around the head of his shaft. Terrance groaned.

"Ooh shit." He immediately pulled over to a vacant parking lot.

"Come on. Suck this shit."

She sat up and reversed the roles on him. "What you gone do for me?"

He placed his hand behind her head and tried to force her head back into his lap. Her cell phone rang causing her to put him on pause. She looked at the caller i.d. and smiled.

"Hold on, baby. Hello?"

Dawn smiled on the other end of the line. "Hey, girl. Do you have anything planned for tomorrow night?"

Mikayla watched Terrance continue to stroke himself. She pulled her bra down and exposed her perky breasts. She played with her nipples and licked her lips.

"You."

Dawn laughed. "You're playing, but that's actually the reason why I called. My man's birthday is tomorrow, and I'd love to give him a double serving of birthday cake."

Mikayla laughed. "Is it really for him or you?"

Dawn smiled. "I won't give you the satisfaction of knowing. He doesn't get off work until ten, so I'll text you my address so we can pregame."

Mikayla picked up the jar and poured herself a bump. "I can't wait. Talk to you later."

She placed the phone back in her purse and inhaled the bump. She watched Terrance continue to stroke himself.

"Since you were such a good boy, you get a treat."

15

Triple Play

Dawn opened the door and invited Mikayla into her home. "Come in."

Mikayla walked in admiring the quaint décor. "It's so cute and cozy in here. I can make myself right at home."

Dawn stood back admiring Mikayla's shape. From her thick thighs to her small waist, she oozed sex. Dawn watched her ass bounce as she walked over to the mantle. She felt Dawn's eyes on her and winked. She turned her attention back to the mantle and ran her fingers across their engagement photos.

"You both look so delicious. This will be fun. Who is this?" she asked, holding up a picture of Dawn, Shannon, and Kenya.

Dawn watched her intensely. "That's my brother and sister."

Mikayla looked at her in shock. "Sister? I thought you were an only child."

Dawn frowned. "When did I tell you that? They are really just my best friends, but my brother passed away. He was killed by a low life piece of shit."

Mikayla's face turned a bright red, and she immediately tried to check her temper. She saw herself smashing the frame and slitting Dawn's throat right then. Instead, she placed the frame down and turned towards Dawn.

"I can't wait to taste you."

Dawn blushed and shifted her weight. "I feel like I've met my match."

Mikayla smiled. "You have."

She walked over to Dawn's bar and poured herself a shot of Hennessy. "Am I drinking alone?"

Dawn walked up to her and grabbed a glass for herself. "Not at all. So where are you from?"

Mikayla hesitated. "…The Dominican Republic."

She'd almost slipped and said Puerto Rico but recovered quickly. She could tell Dawn was extremely intelligent and couldn't risk her connecting the dots and ruining her plans before they'd even been put into motion. She made sure to keep a full face of makeup whenever she was out in public to ensure she looked just like any other racially ambiguous woman. She downed her shot.

"Do you smoke?"

Dawn shook her head no but quickly offered, "But you can. Just go out to the patio.

Mikayla grabbed her hand and pulled her close. "How long do we have before Mr. Officer comes in?"

Dawn checked the time. "Forty-five minutes. It seems I told you a lot about me, but I know nothing about you except your name."

Mikayla squeezed her ass, ignoring her probe.

"Perfect! Show me the patio."

Dawn broke free and walked towards the sliding door. Mikayla already had her pussy dripping, and if that was any indication of what was to come, tonight would be amazing. They walked out to the patio and Dawn hit the switch to turn on the ceiling fan.

Mikayla placed the flame from the lighter to her blunt and inhaled slowly. Dawn was mesmerized by her red lips and watched her exhale the smoke.

"Do you do everything seductively?"

Mikayla laughed. "Are you seduced?"

Dawn, who was always cool, tried to hide her nervousness. "So, I'm thinking that when he comes home, I'll hide you and get in the shower with him. Five minutes after you hear the shower, you can join us."

Mikayla took another deep puff. "Say less. Have y'all done this before?"

Dawn shook her head. "Not together. We've been monogamous, but I'm a free spirit. I've never considered this before, but you're the perfect candidate to introduce to him."

Mikayla stood and put her blunt out on the railing. She walked towards Dawn and backed her into a corner. Dawn licked her lips and her voice trembled. She couldn't tell if it was Mikayla making her act like this or the anticipation of trying something new with her man.

"What are you doing?"

Mikayla silenced her by placing her lips on hers. In a swift movement, Dawn's jeans were unbuttoned, and Mikayla started to massage her clit. Her juices start to drip as she thrust her hips into Mikayla's fingers with a deep moan. Mikayla slipped a finger inside and began to rub across her G Spot while still massaging her clit with her hand. She used her other hand and started to slide her jeans and panties over her ass. Dawn spread her legs to allow her easier access. Mikayla got down on both knees and put her warm mouth on Dawn's clit, sucking it softly into her mouth. Dawn let out a growl and grabbed a handful of Mikayla's hair. She started to ride her face, not realizing that her feet were no longer touching the ground. The doorbell rang, snapping them out of it. Dawn jumped off her face and grabbed her pants. She looked at her watch.

"Damn, it's him. Remember to wait five minutes."

The doorbell rang again. Dawn stuffed her jeans behind the pillow on the couch and opened the door in her panties. Ryan's eyes widened and he grabbed her ass and pulled her into him. She began to unbutton his shirt while he massaged her ass and hips. He released his holster and placed it on the couch beside them. Dawn stuck her tongue in his mouth and wrapped her arms around his neck. She removed his shirt at the same time that he picked her up. She wrapped her legs around his waist while he unzipped his pants and let his dick spring free. He moaned as the seat of her wet panties rubbed across his dick.

"I was wondering why both locks were on and what was taking you so long."

She continued to grind on him and ran her nails down his back. She looked towards the patio and lost it when she saw Mikayla standing there butt naked, rubbing her pussy, and watching them. Dawn moaned.

"Baby, let's go to the shower?"

She held on tightly as he walked towards the bathroom. Dawn removed her shirt and tossed it on the floor, continuously grinding on his dick and soaking her panties. Ryan sucked her right nipple in his mouth and turned the bathroom light on with his elbow. He placed her on her feet and stepped out of his pants that were now around his waist. Then, he bit his lip and watched her naked body turn on the shower. She stepped into the walk-in shower, pulled him in with her, and pressed her breast into his chest.

Mikayla who'd entered the house as soon as they disappeared from sight, stood at the door watching Ryan lift Dawn to his face so that he could taste her. She quietly opened the shower door and walked in, immediately dropping to her knees. She grabbed Ryan's dick, put him in her mouth, and made his entire dick disappear. He moaned, realizing what was happening, and stuck his tongue deep inside of Dawn. Mikayla started to use her hands. Before he could stop it, he released his seed into her mouth. She swallowed and stood.

"Happy Birthday, Big Boy!"

Ryan put Dawn on her feet and looked at her with a shocked expression on his face. He couldn't believe this was really happening. She pulled Mikayla up to her and tongue kissed her while massaging her clit at the same time. Ryan felt like a kid in a candy store.

"Well damn." His eyes roamed over Mikayla's body, and his dick grew hard again. She reached out and started to stroke him as Dawn pushed her towards him. He positioned himself behind Mikayla and slid deep inside of her. She reached for Dawn. "Come here, baby."

She grabbed Dawn's breasts softly and started to suck her nipples simultaneously. They continued to take turns pleasing each other in the shower until they couldn't stand the steam anymore. They moved to the bedroom and didn't come up for air until the sun beamed through the windows and the birds chirped their good morning song.

16
Black Moon

Kenya laughed at Jess's impersonation of the rapper Gates as she put the final pin curl in her client's hair.

"I love him so much. He's my problematic fave."

Brittany nodded her head. "I have to agree with that! He can't do anything wrong in my eyes."

Jess took Brittany's words as encouragement and continued her impersonation. Carla rolled her eyes and interrupted the performance.

"He's an asshole and super disrespectful to women. I can't even listen to his music anymore."

Jess fanned her off. "Do you even listen to rap? I haven't ever heard you singing anything but that incense music."

Carla choked on her water. "Incense music? What the hell are you talking about?"

Jess motioned for her client. "You know what I'm talking about. That type of music that makes you turn the lights off, light some candles and incense, and sit Indian style on the floor."

Carla frowned but ended up laughing. "A whole entire vibe, honey. Get into it!"

Duane's client raised her hand and waited to be called on. He laughed loudly, giving everyone else the okay to join in. "Girl, you aren't in damn school! What's up?"

Stacy laughed. "Okay, I have a question. I have a friend whose boyfriend brought home a vibrator to spice up their sex life. She thought he was about to try something freaky like double penetration or something. Well, when it was time and the vibrator came out, he handed it to her and got on all fours. Is that gay?"

The woman shouted out, "Gay!"

Kenya shook her head in disagreement. "That is not gay! You're a woman. Nothing that he does with you is gay."

Duane walked up to her and gave her a high five. "Thank you, Kenya, You're the only one in here with common sense. Now, if you had said something like 'I found Duane's number in his phone and saw where he keeps sending him black moon emojis,' we could have had a conversation"

Stacy's face turned white as it registered in her brain. "Wait…what?"

Duane put his hand in the position as though he was sipping tea. "I'm just saying, child. We met him on the same day. He slipped me his number just like he slipped it to you… I mean *your friend.*"

Stacy stood up and turned around to face Duane. "You mean you've been sleeping with my man?"

He laughed and picked up his curling iron, prepared to use it as a weapon. "I'm saying that's everybody's man, and the only option he had was to get a vibrator because I don't want him."

Stacy snatched the cape from around her neck. "Fuck you, Duane! You can have that sorry piece of shit because I don't want him!"

She stormed towards the exit, ignoring the looks from the women and laughter that filled the shop. She flipped Duane off and hurriedly pushed the door open but was not quick enough to miss him yelling out, "He doesn't want you either girl!"

Jess swung her cape and tied it around her client's neck. "Darla, you sure are glowing! What's been up with you? What do you want me to do? It looks like I just cut your hair this morning."

Darla laughed and ran her manicured fingernails through her tapered curls. "You know your girl has to stay fly. Just a little off the top today. I think I just met my future wife, so I definitely have to stay on point.

Jess laughed. "You keep a new one on your arm. I'm sure she's bad. Let me see her."

Darla pulled her phone from her clutch. "She's so different from anyone I've ever dated, but I'm falling for her ass."

Jess brushed the sides of her taper down. "Oh yeah? Different like how?"

Darla tapped her nails on her phone screen as she unlocked it and searched for a picture of her new boo. "She's a little more dominant than I'm used to but real corporate. She's older, in her thirties with no kids, and she's never been married. She's been helping me get my demo together, which I'm so excited about. I've been to her studio every day since I met her."

Kenya's ears started to burn, and she instantly got a headache. She sized Darla up. "Do you sing or rap?"

Darla smiled. "I'm a singer."

Jess picked up on the tension in Kenya's voice and pressed Darla for a picture again. "Mane, you sound like you're in love. Let me see her."

Kenya's heart started to beat extremely fast, and she almost walked over to see the picture, too. Darla held the phone up and Jess laughed. "Y'all real cute together."

Jess looked at Kenya and shook her head no, putting her nerves at ease. Kenya exhaled and mouthed. "Thank you."

~

They finished another karaoke song and the crowd erupted in applause. Dawn, the most intoxicated, stopped in the middle of the floor and took a bow. Several men whistled, and the women cheered her on. Kenya walked back to their table laughing at her friend soaking up all the attention. She grabbed her water bottle and took a huge gulp.

"Whew, that song takes a lot out of you. I don't know how she can perform multiple nights in a row for hours. One song almost took me out!"

Dawn flagged the waitress down for another margarita. "Do you want one, Natalie?"

Natalie applied another coat of lipstick. "Hell, yea I want another one. I just sweated my buzz out." The waitress motioned to Kenya. "Do you want another one, too?"

Kenya shook her head no. "I'll take another water. Thank you."

Dawn frowned and motioned to Kenya. "I should have known you were going to say no. That's why I didn't ask. You never do anything with me anymore."

Dawn's comment caught her completely off guard, especially since there was a little aggression in her voice. Kenya blamed it on the tequila but decided to press her anyway.

"What is that supposed to mean? How do I not do anything with you anymore, and I'm here with you tonight?"

Natalie attempted to calm whatever this was that was bubbling up, knowing that her cousin had drunk maybe one too many margaritas.

"What's the next song that y'all want to do?

Dawn ignored her and continued her rant. "This is the happiest time of my life, and my supposedly best friend is nowhere to be found. The only reason why you probably agreed to come here tonight was so that you could see Taylor. I'm always there for you, but when are you ever there for me? You don't even know what's been going on in my life."

Kenya laughed. "I don't think you should drink another margarita. It seems like you have hit your limit. I'm not able to get up and go every time you want to go out, Dawn. I'm a mother."

Dawn's eyes teared up. "So now you want to throw that in my face? I know that I'll never be a mother, Kenya, but at least my man still loves me. Where's yours, huh? When's the last time you saw her? The last time I saw her was in the club last night with a bitch that wasn't you."

People around them started to look in their direction and Kenya stood. "What do you mean you saw her in the club?"

Natalie grabbed Dawn by the hand. "Come on, let's go outside for some air."

Dawn allowed Natalie to lead her towards the exit. Kenya followed close on their heels. As soon as they stepped outside, the cold night air hit them all. Everyone shivered except Kenya whose blood was boiling.

"What do you mean you saw her at the club last night? Kai is supposed to be in Houston."

Dawn laughed. "Not unless she can be in two places at once. You don't know shit!"

Kenya looked at Natalie. "I know she's full of liquid courage right now. Were you with her last night? Was Kai at the club?"

Dawn yelled before Natalie could respond. "Don't yell at my cousin! She isn't the one you should be questioning."

Mikayla stood in the shadow of the doorway and laughed at the women as they tore each other apart with their words. *This shit is better than anything I could have done. It's go time!*

17

Bigger Than Us

Kenya dialed Kai's number again. She'd been calling her since she left the restaurant last night but had no luck. Her voicemail picked up once again. This time she decided to leave a message.

"Kai, I know that we haven't talked. I also know that the last time we talked, you were speaking from anger. The court hearing is today at 11. I texted and told you this last week, but you never responded. I hope that you show up today. This is bigger than us; this is about our son."

Kenya ended the call, placed her phone down, and walked into Dre's room. She couldn't believe that she was about to go to court to fight for her own child. She stood at his door and watched him sleeping so peacefully.

"Don't worry, baby. I will protect you at any cost," she whispered.

She walked out of his room, softly closing the door behind her. She went to the kitchen and poured herself a cup of coffee. As she sipped the freshly brewed goodness, she glanced at the clock and realized that it was 9:15 a.m. She gathered her things when she saw Maria's car pull into the driveway. Then, she met her at the door to stop her from ringing the doorbell.

"Good morning, Mrs. Johnson."

Kenya smiled. "Good morning, Maria. Thank you for coming so early. I'll be back as soon as possible. He's still asleep, but when he awakens, give him any cereal he wants."

Maria smiled her usual pleasant smile and stood at the door until Kenya was inside her car. Kenya hit the button to dial Kai's number again. She was shocked when she answered. Her raspy voice was evidence that she was still sleeping.

"Hello?"

Kenya suppressed her irritation from hearing Kai still asleep. "Kai, did you get any of my messages? Are you coming to the hearing?"

The phone got silent. "Who is this?"

Kenya checked her display screen in her car to make sure she hadn't dialed the wrong number. "Kai, wake up. This is Kenya!"

Silence, again. Kenya exhaled loudly. "Hello! Kai?"

"Kai's still sleeping. Call her back later."

Before Kenya could ask who was answering Kai's phone, the line disconnected. She choked back her tears and put her game face on. A tiny little voice in the back of her head reminded her that if she had a Xanax all of her anxiety would go away, but she quickly dismissed that thought. *Never again. My baby deserves at least one stable parent.* Her GPS alerted her that she'd arrived at the courthouse as she pulled into the parking lot. She parked, said a protection prayer, and exited the car. She went to the parking meter and paid for half a day. *I don't know how long this is going to take.*

After gaining clearance through the metal detectors at the entrance of the building, she entered the courtroom her case was assigned to and grabbed an empty bench in the back. She sat nervously picking at her fingernail polish as she watched a lady fight for sole custody of her daughters. She was pleading her case that she was the only one who could keep them safe from their abusive father. Dawn and Ryan walked up to her bench, forcing her from her thoughts. She slid down to give them room. Dawn immediately grabbed her hand and squeezed it.

"I'm so sorry about last night."

Kenya placed her hand on top of Dawn's. "Families fight. Thank you for coming."

Dawn rolled her eyes and sternly whispered.

"That's my godson! Why wouldn't I be here?" She leaned forward and looked around Kenya.

"Where is Kai?"

Kenya shrugged and frowned. "I keep asking myself the same question."

Dawn glanced at the lawyer Kenya had just greeted. "Why didn't you use Charles? I thought you said he was on retainer."

Kenya smoothed the invisible wrinkles from her skirt. "He was…booked."

She couldn't deal with trying to explain to Dawn how Kai had once again turned her back on her family. Dawn recognized the look on Kenya's face but decided not to probe.

"How'd you find her?"

"I've been doing her hair for the last six years."

Dawn nodded. "Ok cool. So, she knows you on a personal level."

They listened as the judge granted sole custody to the mother in the best interest of the children. That verdict eased Kenya's nerves a tad and she excitedly gathered her briefcase as her lawyer, Nicole, waved her to the defendant table. She hugged Dawn and whispered in her ear, "Say a prayer for us."

18

Performing Arts

"All rise."

Everyone stood and waited for the judge to walk into the courtroom. Kenya's calmed nerves instantly went through the roof when she saw that it was a different judge. Nicole's string of whispered curse words did nothing to reverse that.

"Court is now in session for the honorable Judge Matthew Bowers."

She whispered to Nicole. "What's the problem? What happened to the other judge?"

Nicole shrugged. "I knew it was a 50/50 chance we'd get him, but I thought we'd dodged him. If there's anything that Lena can say that would make you seem unfit, you'd better tell me now so I can postpone!"

Kenya turned and looked at Dawn nervously.

Dawn mouthed, "You got this."

She turned back around quickly when Judge Bowers called Lena to the stand. Kenya burned holes into her back when she hobbled to the front like a decrepit old woman. Kenya's leg shook angrily as Lena, who the bailiff was currently swearing-in, never took her eyes off her. The judge asked her to state her name and relation to the child in question.

"I'm Lena Diane Duncan, and I am that child's grandmother."

Kenya leaned in and whispered to her lawyer, forcing Lena to shoot her a menacing glare. The judge rustled a few sheets of paper. "

Allegedly."

Lena pursed her lips and smiled at the judge. "Yes. Sorry, your honor. I believe I am his grandmother."

Unbeknownst to everyone in the courtroom, Lena had already conducted her own DNA test from the hair she'd collected when she visited him at school. She knew for a fact that Dre was her grandchild. *You should have chosen a better school you, nasty bull-dagger. It was too simple to get them to call him out of class.* The judge repeated his question when Lena failed to answer.

"You are petitioning for joint custody if the court finds that this is your biological grandchild, is that correct?"

Lena nodded her head, never breaking eye contact with Kenya. "Yes."

"Is there anything additional that you would like to tell the court besides the motion that your lawyer has already submitted?"

Lena finally averted her eyes and started to weep.

"Your honor, it was already tough when my son was brutally murdered but to find out it was her ex-boyfriend that did it was like experiencing his death all over again. She was supposed to be Shannon's best friend. To find out she was behind his murder…"

Lena started to cry hysterically. Kenya's lawyer stood hurriedly.

"Objection, your honor! My client's involvement with the person who murdered her son has nothing to do with the paternity of the child. There is no evidence being submitted from that statement. My client was also a victim of this same person."

The judge faced Lena. "Is there a reason that you are bringing up Mrs. Johnson's prior dating history? Is it relevant to your plea?"

Lena dabbed at her crocodile tears. "Yes, your honor. I believe that her involvement with that murderer is one of the first clues of the unstableness that is her life."

Judge Bowers faced Kenya's lawyer. "I'll allow it. Please continue."

Lena smirked triumphantly. "She used my son's sperm without his expressed permission, and…allegedly conceived this child with it. My son never got a chance to know his child. She didn't even have the decency to let me know there was a child. I saw him out with the man who used to physically and verbally abuse my son."

"Objection your honor. Ms. Duncan is speaking from hearsay. The man in question is not here to defend himself against these claims."

Judge Bowers nodded. "The court will strike that from the record. Ms. Duncan, you may continue, and please stick to facts."

Lena again dabbled at her fake tears. "I asked her personally if I was this child's grandmother and the lying… I'm sorry. She lied to my face and flat out said no. The child is currently not in a stable environment."

She made eye contact with Kenya again. Kenya became nauseous from the smile in her eyes.

"I know she's going to think that it has something to do with her being in a relationship with a woman, but that's not it at all. I have a gay son... had..."

Lena's tearful theatrics continued. "I know for a fact that she leaves him with a babysitter at least five times out of the week. All I'm asking for is the time to get the child neither my son nor I knew anything about. I can give him the stability that he is currently missing being around all these homo-different people of no relation."

The judge wrote down a couple of notes. "Thank you, Ms. Duncan."

Once again, Lena moved slowly as she walked from the stand back to the plaintiff's table with her lawyer. Kenya watched her intensely. *This lady is really an actress.* Judge Bowers asked for the bailiff to hand him the results of the paternity test. Kenya sat calmly. This was the part that wouldn't catch her off guard. In hindsight, she wished that she'd just told Lena the truth but didn't think it would have gone this far.

"In the case of Shannon Deandre Johnson-Sanchez, DNA test results show that you and the child share genetic markers, Ms. Duncan. Unfortunately, we weren't able to test the father. However, Mrs. Johnson-Sanchez, being completely transparent, advises the court that she did indeed use Shannon's sperm for conception."

Lena gasped and set Kenya on fire with her eyes. Judge Bowers continued, "Mrs. Johnson, do you have anything that you'd like to say before the court renders a decision?"

Kenya stood and smoothed her jacket and skirt down. "I do, your honor."

She walked towards the stand and took a seat. The bailiff swore her in, and she waited for the judge. "You may begin."

Kenya looked in Lena's direction. "One thing that she was right about was Shannon being my best friend. The 'little friend' that she's speaking of was Shannon's husband, and he's also the godfather of my child. Dre…my son, Shannon, is extremely loved and protected. I received permission from Shannon's husband to use the sperm."

Kenya's lawyer stood. "Your honor, I would like to enter this notarized letter from Shannon's widow into evidence."

Lena stood quickly, knocking her chair against the railing behind her table. "Objection, your honor!"

Judge Bowers looked over the top of his glasses. "What exactly are you objecting?"

Lena's lawyer stood. "We are objecting, the uh…" He leaned over and allowed Lena to whisper something in his ear. Her words must have cut deep because his face turned beet red.

"We are objecting Mrs. Johnson tarnishing Shannon's name. He does not have a widow."

Nicole grabbed another document from her briefcase. "Your honor, may I please approach the bench?"

The judge motioned for both counselors to approach. Nicole, who'd regained her confidence, handed Judge Bowers two documents.

"Your honor, there's no tarnishing. This marriage license was submitted into evidence previously because Shannon's husband gave permission to my client."

She handed a copy of the notarized letter to Lena's lawyer.

"Bob, I know your client doesn't want to believe her son was married to a man, but you had the proof."

Judge Bowers looked into the crowd. "This document will be accepted as evidence. Counselor Briggs, I expect no more outbursts from your client, or I will hold her in contempt."

He motioned for Kenya to continue. She bit the inside of her lip. "I know that I should have been honest when she asked if he was her grandchild, but I panicked. Many nights, I've consoled Shannon who was often the victim of her homophobic rants."

"Objection! Speculation."

Irritation was beginning to show on Judge Bowers' face. "Overruled."

He motioned for Kenya to continue. She looked in Lena's direction.

"My son is being raised in love, and I never want him to feel bad about who he is no matter what that may be."

Judge Bowers excused Kenya. "You may be seated."

He waited until she sat before he continued. "I have heard both of your arguments and reviewed the evidence. It is under my belief that if the biological father were still alive, he would have been in the child's life. There is nothing legally in writing that waives the Duncan family rights to the child. Custody is granted to the paternal grandmother for one weekend a month."

19
Family Ties

Mikayla walked down the gravel road towards Micah's grave. She stopped at the entrance and took a deep breath. She hadn't seen her brother in years and definitely didn't think this would be the next time they'd see each other. She walked up to his grave and looked over his tombstone. He'd had a basic grave marker, but she'd made sure to get a tombstone worthy of him.

"Hey, bighead!"

A gust of wind caused her hair to blow in her face.

"I know. I'm happy to see you, too. I'm going to sit on your lap okay?"

She waited for some type of response until she realized she was being silly. She sat with her legs tucked under her and leaned her head back to rest it on the tombstone.

"I still can't believe that you're no longer here."

Mikayla wiped at the tears that formed in her eyes.

"It pisses me off, Mick! I think back to the day you met that bitch. I told you I hated her. Brandi was the girl you were supposed to be with. I set it up perfectly and had her head over heels for you!"

Mikayla thought back to the times before Micah transitioned. They were identical and got a kick out of trading lives. They'd done it since they were children, usually to save Mikayla from some type of trouble she'd gotten into.

"I guess the poetic thing is that you're both together right now if she isn't still mad at you for killing her."

A butterfly fluttered around her head, and she laughed. That had always been the name she called Brandi. Mikayla remembered telling her, *wait until you go into your cocoon. You're going to come out as a beautiful butterfly.*

"Hey, Brandi! I guess you know the truth now, huh? I'm sorry that we tricked you, but you deserved to be loved. My knucklehead brother didn't understand what he had. He was stuck on that bitch and look at all the trouble she caused."

The butterfly flew around her head as if acknowledging her apology before it flew away. "Ugh! I miss you both so much. I constantly ask myself all the time what you saw in her, and I still don't know. She's so fucking annoying!"

She stopped talking and waved back at a family walking past. She waited until they were out of view before she continued.

"I do have to admit that she has some good pussy, though. Maybe that's what made you lose all your good sense! I used to wonder why you transitioned before I understood. I always thought it was to keep me from being mean to her. 'Cause you'd always come back like captain save a hoe and buy her something."

Thunder rolled and caused her to look up into the sky.

"Calm down. You never could handle the truth. I just wanted to talk to you and let you know that I will forever be indebted to you. That's why it was such a pleasure to receive your go-ahead on torturing that bitch. Thank you for everything that you've ever done for me, bro! I'll see you soon."

A raindrop hit her in the face and rolled down her cheek like a tear. She stood and placed the rose that she'd been holding onto the grave. Just then, her cell phone rang. She paused before answering.

"What the hell?"

Mikayla watched the Puerto Rico number scroll across her screen.

"Hello?"

A man with a thick Spanish accent replied. "Hello, may I speak to Micah?"

Mikayla turned and glanced at the grave. "Micah's not available, but this is his sister Mikayla. How can I help you?"

The man screamed into the phone. "Oh, my God! Mikayla, Hola', Señorita! When did you get out?"

Mikayla was taken aback that the man seemed to know her so well. "Who is this?"

The man chuckled. "It's your Tio, Javier."

Mikayla gasped. "You're my uncle? Whose brother are you? How did you get this number?"

Javier laughed again. "I talk to Micah all the time. I'm your papa's baby brother. I haven't talked to him in a while because your abuela's been so sick. That's actually the reason for my call today. She is ready to transition but will not stop asking to see you both. Is there any way you can come? I'll get the tickets."

Mikayla was quiet from shock.

Javi laughed. "I know it's a lot, Mija, and there's so much that you both need to know. Can you leave tomorrow? I'll buy the tickets right now!"

Mikayla sat back down on Micah's grave. She couldn't believe what she was hearing. She didn't even know her father's family knew about her. "Micah's dead."

Javi blew into the phone. "Damn. I'll light a candle."

Mikayla waited for him to break the silence. Javi said nothing. Mikayla laughed. *I guess our stubbornness came from my dad's side.*

"I can leave tomorrow."

Javi laughed again. "Perfect! Grab a pen and paper. I'm purchasing your ticket now. Flight leaves at 5:45 a.m."

Mikayla ended the call after saving the confirmation number in the notes on her phone. A lightning strike lit up the sky followed by a loud roll of thunder. She looked at Micah's grave.

"You always were the sneaky one!"

Rain started to pour out of the sky. She yelled out, "I love you, Micah!" as she raced back to her car.

20

Reality Check

Kenya sat at the dining room table sipping a glass of Merlot while going over the books for her salon. Her leg shook nervously as she waited to see Kai's truck pull into the driveway. Kai had just called her to say that she needed to get something out of her home office and would be over soon. She glanced at her watch. *12:15 p.m.* She was glad that Dre was in school so she wouldn't have to deal with the joy of him seeing his mother and thinking she was coming home. She was pissed about Kai not coming to court and even more upset that she thought she could just casually show up. It had been weeks since she last saw her, and the hairs standing up on the back of her neck warned that this meeting wouldn't be pleasant. She finished her glass and poured herself another filled to the rim.

The doorbell rang and startled her as she hadn't seen Kai pull into the driveway. She walked towards the front door and was glad that she'd put the chain up and Kai couldn't use her key. She stopped at the door and checked herself in the mirror before opening it. Kai stood there looking good as hell in a pair of jeans and a white wife-beater. Her hair was pulled up into a high messy bun and she smelled amazing. Kenya stepped back to allow her to enter and moved away when Kai tried to place a kiss on her cheek. She walked to the table and picked up her wine glass, ignoring Kai as she watched her.

"Day drinking? In those little ass shorts... What have you been doing?"

Kenya finished her glass in record timing again. "I need to be asking what the hell you've been doing. Why didn't you show up to court?"

Kai exhaled. "I've been super busy...with work. It slipped my mind. How'd it go?"

Kenya hiccupped, feeling the consequences of drinking her wine so fast. "I lost. She got visitation. I called you that morning to remind you, but your lil girlfriend answered your phone."

Kai looked at her in confusion. "Girlfriend? Man, here you go again. Every time I'm around you, you come up with something else to start drama."

Kenya's voice raised quickly. "Fuck you, Kai! You walked out on me and Dre! On your vows! How dare you stand there and tell me about drama. You haven't been home in two months. And when I do get the nerves to call, I have to talk to another woman about my wife...my wife, Kai! What happened to the promise you made me?"

Kai stood against the wall staring at her. "I don't know if it's the wine or your vulnerability, but I'm so turned on. Can I have some of my pussy?"

Kenya screamed. "It's not a joke, Kai! I don't know why you think this is a joke. It's obvious that you don't care about anything but what you want. So get your shit and get out of my house!"

Kai walked towards her. "Your house? Who do you think you're talking to?"

Kenya stepped back and accidentally bumped into the dining room table. "What are you going to do, Kai? Hit me? You are not the person I fell in love with! I've wasted all these fucking years on you."

Kai walked towards her again, this time backing Kenya up against the wall.

"I am different, but you are, too. That's what people do, Kenya. They change!"

Kai took another step towards her. This time she was so close that Kenya could feel her breath on her face. "You know you miss me! Stop playing hard."

Kenya squirmed in an attempt to break their closeness but was caught off guard as Kai pinned her arms above her against the wall. She leaned in and kissed Kenya on her neck. "Chill out. What can I do to make it better? I want you."

Kenya's wine-impaired brain betrayed her as she leaned into Kai. "I'm so mad at you. It's like I don't even know who you are anymore. You can tell me anything, Kai, but you can't just treat me like I'm any old thing."

Kai placed a trail of kisses down to her left breast. "I'm *kiss* still *kiss* me *kiss.*"

The warmth from Kai's mouth instantly caused the seat of her shorts to get soaked. Her breath caught in her throat. "Kai, what are you doing?"

Kai slid Kenya's shorts down and then slid her hand between her legs and began massaging her clit.

"I want you to taste me. Don't you miss my taste."

Against her better judgment, Kenya nodded her head yes. Kai unfastened her belt buckle and slid her pants and boxer briefs down to her ankles before stepping out of them. Kenya followed the curves of her hips and long legs and bit her lip. Kai jumped up on the counter and pulled Kenya close to her. Kenya attempted to kiss her lips, but Kai pushed her head down towards her open legs.

"Kiss me there."

Kenya got down on her knees and inhaled Kai's aroma while sucking her clit into her mouth. She started to alternate slipping her tongue inside of Kai and softly sucking her clit into her mouth. Kai started to buck her hips as she rode Kenya's mouth. Kenya reached around her and grabbed her ass as she pulled her closer. That seemed to push Kai to the edge as her body started to convulse.

"Oh, shit! I'm coming."

She wrapped her legs around Kenya's neck and held on until her body stopped shaking. As soon as she released her from the grip of her legs, Kenya stood up. She looked at Kai with a satisfied expression on her face.

"It seemed like you really needed that. I guess I did miss you, too. When are you coming home?"

Kai hopped off the counter and picked her pants and underwear up. Kenya watched her with a perplexed expression on her face.

"Give them to me. I'm about to do a load of clothes anyway."

Kai stepped into her underwear without ever acknowledging anything Kenya said. Kenya's head started to spin, and she couldn't tell if it was the wine or the anger bubbling up inside of her.

"What are you doing? Where are you going?!"

Kai looked at her with a half-smile on her face.

"I'm going home."

Kenya frowned while grabbing her shorts putting them back on.

"What do you mean? You are at home. Where the fuck is home if it's not here?"

Kai grabbed her keys. "Look, Kenya. We had a little fun, but I don't love you anymore. I don't want this. We are over."

Kenya picked up her wine glass and hurled it at Kai's head, barely missing.

"Get the fuck out of my house you piece of shit. I hate you!"

Kai laughed and blew Kenya an air kiss. "Gladly."

21

Whatever You Need

"Hello. May I speak to Taylor?"

"Speaking. What's going on, Ms. Kenya?"

Kenya smiled. She was happy to hear a friendly voice on the other end. She'd been focusing on spending as much time as possible with Dre, but tonight she needed a little adult conversation.

"Did you know my voice, or did you have my number saved? You crossed my mind, and I wanted to reach out."

Taylor sat back on her couch and kicked her feet back. "Lucky me! I saved your number the first day you gave it to me. Where's your family?"

Kenya turned the volume on her television down. "My son's asleep." She glanced at the clock. "It is 9:43 p.m. and a school night."

Taylor laughed. "Oh yeah. My bad. I don't have kids, so I always forget that sort of thing. Where's your wife?"

Kenya frowned. Kai was the last thing she wanted to talk about tonight. She quickly redirected the conversation.

"So, where do you live?"

Taylor picked up on the hint that there was trouble on the home front. She slowed her breathing and prepared to slide in. "I stay on the island by Max's Grill."

Kenya exhaled; she was grateful that she didn't live close. "Oh, so you stay on the other side of town. Cool. What kind of work do you do?"

Taylor hesitated before answering. "I'm a…ah, Dom dancer."

Kenya laughed. "A Dom dancer? What is that?!"

Taylor bit the inside of her lip. "That wasn't a joke. I'm a dominant exotic dancer."

Kenya quickly realized that she wasn't playing. Her mind instantly flashed an image of Taylor in a G-string. *Sexy.*

"Oh, I didn't mean any harm. I didn't know what you meant. How long have you danced?"

Taylor paused as if she was counting. "You know what… Saturday will actually make seven years."

Kenya chuckled to herself as the visual image of Taylor slow winding continued to play in her head. She came to the realization that she actually did have a type. Taylor was average height, about 5'7" with light skin, long locs, and an athletic build.

"Well, happy early anniversary. How are you celebrating?"

Taylor decided to shoot her shot. Kenya had chosen to call her for a reason, so she knew that she'd be crazy not to take advantage.

"I haven't really thought about it. Would you like to go out and celebrate with me?"

Kenya paused. *What if someone sees us? I know Kai said some hurtful things, but that's still my wife. Why did I call this woman?* Kai's words replayed in her head. *I don't love you anymore!*

"I don't really go out anymore," she lied.

Taylor laughed silently. "You don't go out anymore? Literally, every time I've seen you, you've been out. You just mean you don't want to go out with me?"

Kenya frowned. "Honestly, Taylor, you know that I'm married – even if we aren't in the best place."

Taylor rolled her eyes in disappointment. "I get it. What if you come over and cook for me?"

Kenya laughed. "Cook for you? Why can't you cook for me?"

Taylor rubbed her hand across her mouth and cupped her chin. "It's my anniversary, Ms. Kenya."

Kenya smiled. "Oh yeah. I forgot that quick." "Ah, that's cold."

Kenya was enjoying the flirting and decided to push it one step further. "What you going to do for me if I come over and cook?"

Taylor visualized Kenya's naked bod and sucked her bottom lip. "You'll just have to cook and see."

Kenya bit the inside of her jaw nervously, and the phone grew increasingly silent. "Saturday at 8 p.m.?"

Taylor licked her lips. "Netflix and chill it is." Kenya laid back on her couch and put her feet up against the wall like a schoolgirl.

"How old are you?"

"Twenty-five."

"Humph."

Taylor frowned. "What does the humph mean?"

Kenya chuckled. "You're a baby."

Taylor's cockiness kicked in. "Yeah okay. You can think I'm a baby. You'll see."

Kenya flirted right back. "I can't wait. When's your birthday?"

Taylor laughed. "You're into zodiacs, too? I'm an Aquarius."

Kenya inhaled sharply. "Yikes!"

"You have jokes tonight?"

"Nope. It explains why you're so charming. Aquarius people usually have lots of game."

"Well, are you ready Player 2?"

Kenya redirected again. "Will I have to worry about a girlfriend showing up while I'm there?"

"I'm single single!"

Kenya exhaled. "I've just been so stressed and could really use a friend."

"I'll be everything you need me to be."

Dre yelled out "Mommy" and startled Kenya.

"Hey, Taylor, my kid just woke up. I need to go check on him. I'll talk to you later."

Taylor smiled. "I'll text you my address. See you soon, beautiful."

22
Whose Family?

Mikayla stepped off the plane with her stomach in knots. She'd always been fearless and confident in herself, but right now she was the total opposite. Yesterday she thought that she was the last person in the world who cared about her; today she knew that was a lie. Her mother had made them believe their father's family wanted nothing to do with them because they were biracial. However, her uncle's call quickly erased those thoughts. As she walked towards baggage claim, she heard someone yell her name.

"Mikayla!"

She turned and stared into the face of the man with a huge perfect smile. He had huge blueish-green eyes with dark features.

"He looks just like Papa. Oh, my God" she said aloud to herself.

They stared at each other and communicated through their silence. Javier seemed to come out of his trance.

"You look just like mama except with brown eyes. That's right. Micah was the one with blue eyes."

Mikayla nodded her head in agreement. "Like yours…and Papa's."

She reached for her luggage and didn't protest when Javi reached for it before she could grab it.

"Our driver is waiting. Follow me."

Mikayla's brow wrinkled. "Driver?"

Javi laughed but didn't answer her as they walked through the doors of the terminal. The driver stood at the back door of a black Escalade with limousine tint. As they approached the vehicle, he walked towards them and retrieved the luggage. Mikayla stood beside her uncle and wondered why they were waiting to enter the SUV. Then, she quickly realized they were waiting for the driver to open the door. He placed the luggage in the trunk and sprinted to them. Once the door was open, Javi motioned for Mikayla to enter.

"After you."

Mikayla glanced at him when the driver said something to him in Spanish. When Javi raised his voice, she hated that she'd never learned Spanish. The only word she'd picked out was *Señor* which didn't offer any context clues. As they traveled to their destination, she looked out the window at the beautiful colorful buildings they'd passed.

"It's so pretty. The news would make you think it looks like ruins over here."

Javi chuckled. "Even our most dangerous cities are beautiful."

Mikayla was mesmerized by the ocean surrounding them. "What is this place called?"

Javier looked out the window. "Oh, this is La Perla. This part is considered the most dangerous because of the high crime rate."

Mikayla stared out the window again. She couldn't imagine anything bad happening here because La Perla looked like paradise. They pulled up to a wooden gate with the name Sanchez scribed in gold across it. A guard in plain clothes stood at the call booth and motioned for the driver to stop. He looked through the driver's window and nodded at Javi. Then, he leaned into the booth and pressed a button to open the gate. The gate opened slowly and exposed a beautiful estate surrounded by pools and fountains. Mikayla's mouth dropped and Javier watched as she took in her surroundings.

"Where are we? This is amazing! I'm staying at a resort?"

Javier laughed deep from within his belly so much that Mikayla joined in. "No resort, Mami. This is the family home."

Mikayla looked at him shocked. "Whose family?"

This sent him into a laughing fit again. The driver joined in this time as he pressed a button on the steering wheel that opened a garage door. They pulled into the garage next to two more Escalades.

"How many people live here?"

Javier opened the door on his side of the vehicle and stepped out.

"Just a few."

Mikayla climbed out of the truck and smiled when they were rushed by at least seven small children engulfing them in hugs and giggles. Javier introduced each one of her cousins by name. Her youngest cousin, Marigold, who they called Mari grabbed her hand and led her into the house. *I'm never leaving this place,* she thought to herself. She walked into a kitchen that was the size of her entire apartment and then into the foyer where she was overwhelmed with more hugs and kisses. She was introduced to more cousins, her aunts, and her grandmother Evelyn who wouldn't take her eyes off of her. Even in old age, she was a beautiful, regal woman. Her demeanor clearly showed that she was the matriarch of this family. She was small and almost frail as she sat in the Lazy Boy recliner in the living room but her presence filled the room. Mikayla felt as if Evelyn was looking into her soul with those same bluish-green eyes that many others in the family shared.

"Mija!"

She motioned for Mikayla to come closer. Alba her cousin, another one those piercing eyes, followed closely to translate. Her grandmother grabbed her hand and squeezed. Mikayla felt all the love in the world at that moment. Her grandmother started to speak, and she looked at Alba who immediately began translating.

"I love you just as much as any other person in this room. My blood runs through you and your sisters. Your father was my firstborn, and even when he dishonored the family, I still loved him."

Mikayla tensed up, assuming she was about to call them 'the dishonesty.' Her grandmother squeezed tighter.

"No, girl. You were a blessing. The woman he chose to marry, Camila Flores, was from a rival family. Marrying her put our entire family at risk, but Juan was convinced that it was a union that would make us stronger."

Her grandmother started to have a coughing fit, and Javi ran to her with a glass of water.

"Drink, mama."

Her grandmother fanned him off and continued.

"I begged him not to marry her. I knew she was trouble the first time I saw her, but when she had my grandson, I had no choice but to embrace her for Kaleb's sake."

She studied Mikayla's face and continued when she realized that she wasn't in shock to learn she had a brother.

"When Juan met your mother, Isabela, it was love at first sight. He was conflicted because of his marriage but was ready to end everything when she got pregnant. Camila found out she was pregnant and threatened Juan. We never found out what she said to him exactly, but your mother moved into our home until she gave birth."

Mikayla's jaw clenched, and she looked around at her family. "I was born here?"

Evelyn listened as Alba translated before she continued.

"Yes. You lived here until the age of three."

Mikayla closed her eyes and leaned her head back. "But my birth certificate says that we were born in America."

Evelyn called out to someone who walked up to her with a small gold box that they placed in her lap. Evelyn rubbed the top of the box but didn't open it.

"Your birth certificate was forged. Your papa was accused of stealing a million dollars from Camila's family one month after you were born. So they fled to America but not before making a deal with your mother in exchange for your safety and hers."

Mikayla massaged her temples. "What kind of deal?"

Evelyn opened the box and handed her a birth certificate. Mikayla read over the paper and looked into her grandmother's face.

"What does this mean? Why does it have three girls listed? We were triplets?"

Evelyn laid her head back in the chair. "You are a triplet! Camila experienced a hard pregnancy with Kaleb and was told she'd never have another child. When the million dollars came up missing, she was convinced that Juan had taken it to give to your mother. She gave Juan an ultimatum which included him convincing your mother to give her one of the girls in exchange for protection from her family."

Mikayla's eyes filled with tears. "Kai."

Evelyn nodded her head. "Until you were three years old, your mother dealt with the pain of giving up her child. We helped her get documentation to go to America with you… you and Micah to find Kai and your papa."

Mikayla wiped her tears away as she waited for Evelyn to continue. "Unfortunately, your Papa had already been murdered, and Kai and Kaleb were put into the system."

Evelyn chocked up and her eyes filled with tears. "You have to find Kai and tell her the truth about who you are. Promise me, child."

Mikayla stood and kissed her grandmother on the forehead. "I promise."

Evelyn called for her daughter Rosa.

"I'm ready for bed."

She looked around the room as a man in a light blue scrub uniform appeared. He picked her up and walked towards the stairs, stopping when she tapped his shoulder. Evelyn looked over the room at her children and smiled.

"I love you all."

Mikayla watched as they carried her grandmother up the stairway until she couldn't see her anymore. Javi walked from the kitchen and handed her a shot glass.

"Drink this. Alba, you should take your cousin out to enjoy the town tonight."

He peeled off ten $100 bills and handed the money to her. "Mateo will be your guard tonight."

Mateo appeared, seemingly from the shadows, and adjusted his gun holster. Javi nodded his head as he watched. He placed his hand on the side of Mateo's head.

"Do not let them out of your sight. Whatever happens to them, happens to you."

23
The Nerve

Kenya sat in her car talking to Dawn in the parking lot of the shop.

"Girl, I don't know what the hell is going on with Kai, but she's testing my gangsta."

Dawn smacked her lips. "I know one thing. You're better than me. If Ryan tried some shit like that, I'd cut his dick off."

Kenya sighed. "I don't know. I'm not really mad 'cause she used me. I'm mad that I'm so weak for her. How many times am I supposed to keep forgiving her because we're married?"

The phone got extremely silent. Kenya waved at Jess's wife who was parked as she waited for Jess. Kenya started her car and pulled off. She didn't want any part of the drama about to happen when she realized Jess had already left with Brittany.

"That wasn't a rhetorical question!"

Dawn laughed. "I'm sorry. I was in my own head. I don't know. I don't believe in divorce, so I'm probably not the best person to answer that."

Kenya pulled out of the parking lot. "I guess not. I'm on my way to the house. How far away are you?"

Dawn glanced in the mirror and ran her finger across her forehead. "I'm sitting in your driveway cleaning up my eyebrows."

Kenya cleared her throat. "She's not there is she?"

Dawn laughed. "Nah, Girl. That's the first thing I would have said to you!"

Kenya sighed. "Okay good. I have two hours before I have to pick Dre up from school, and the last thing I need is her showing up again."

Dawn looked at the clock. "You must drive 12 mph. You are the slowest Audi driver I've ever seen. Your shop is literally two minutes away."

Kenya blew her horn, causing Dawn to turn around. "I'd like to get in my driveway. Pull over onto the grass."

Dawn started her car and pulled over to the other lane of the driveway. "Why would I pull into the grass? You need to get your head out of the clouds. I'm hanging up."

Kenya pulled into the garage and turned her car off. Dawn was standing there as soon she opened the door. "Come on and get out. I don't like what this is doing to you."

Kenya unlocked the door, and they walked in with Dawn checking out the surroundings. "At least you're still cleaning."

Kenya laughed. "I'm stressed not depressed. I am trying my best not to throw Dre's routine off. He's the one that's keeping me going. He matters most."

Kenya turned to look for Dawn after she didn't respond and realized she was in the kitchen. She rounded the corner to see Dawn eating a cold piece of fried chicken. "I guess you're glad I'm still cooking, too!"

Dawn laughed, almost choking on her chicken. "Girl, you know I love to eat anyway, but I swear if I could get pregnant, I'd think I was. So, what exactly are we looking for?"

Kenya scratched her head. "Honestly, I don't know. I'm just looking for anything that would explain what's going on with her."

Dawn washed her hands. "Are you sure you want to do this? I can't believe it has really come to this with Kai."

Kenya sighed. "I don't know that I want to do this as much as I feel like I need to. I think her office is the place we need to be."

They walked in Kai's office and stopped at the door. Dawn touched her arm. "It's whatever you want to do. I'm supporting you no matter what you decide."

Kenya looked around at the family photos surrounding the office. "It feels so cold in here. It doesn't even feel like a part of the house."

She focused on a picture of Kai and Dre and wiped at the tears in her eyes. "If it was just me that she was doing like this, I would just let it go, but my baby is innocent."

Dawn grabbed a Kleenex off the desk and handed to her. "I know what you mean. I know that Dre calling Pat 'Papa' didn't do this."

She walked to the desk first. "What's the security code?"

"Dre's Birthday. 0322"

The keypad buzzed and then turned red. Dawn tried again and got the same error. Kenya thought back to the day that she realized the code on Kai's phone was changed. "Try 0704."

Dawn punched in the code, and the keypad turned green, unlocking the drawers.

"That worked. What's that number?"

Kenya bit her lip. "She changed it to her birthday again."

"Again?!"

"Yeah. Everything that was Dre's Birthday is now hers. So fitting... She only cares about herself now. What's in the drawer?"

Dawn moved somethings around. "Nothing. Just this old newspaper."

She picked the newspaper up to show her and a chalky white powdery substance fell out followed by a clear baggy. She looked at Kenya with remorse. "Selling or using?"

24

We Just Want to Have Fun

Mateo pulled up to the entrance, blocking the crowd waiting in line to get into the club. He turned and looked at Alba and Mikayla.

"Wait here."

He stepped out of the car, ignoring questions from the club-goers trying to figure out who was in the back of the car. Mikayla could hear the bass from the reggae-ton song currently playing inside the club, thumping the windows of the SUV. Moments later, Mateo and a burly looking bouncer walked towards the car side by side. Mateo opened Mikayla's door and motioned for both women to step out to the red carpet that led to the entrance. Mikayla stepped out and waited for Alba to apply a fresh coat of lipstick. Once she was satisfied with her look, Alba stepped out and blew a kiss to the line of people waiting to enter the club. To Mikayla's surprise, the crowd cheered and waved back. Mikayla leaned into Alba.

"Are you some kind of celebrity?"

Alba grabbed her hand and led her towards the entrance. "We're just part of the Sanchez family. We are well respected in this town."

Mateo stepped to the side of the bouncers and pointed towards VIP. Alba kissed his cheek and walked into their Private section. The scantily-clad server Angel stood in the area ready to handle anything they threw her way. She smiled at Mikayla who licked her lips when she spoke to them. In a thick Spanish accent, she asked what they'd like to drink. Mikayla turned to Alba for translation and asked for a Hennessy and coke. Angel walked towards the velvet rope and tapped Mateo's shoulder to let her out. Mikayla watched the fabric stretch over her ass and subconsciously licked her lips again. Alba laughed bringing her attention back to her.

"So, you like girls?"

Mikayla nodded her head yes. "…And guys. I just like beautiful people."

A salsa song came on and Alba stood and moved her body to the music. Her long-bronzed legs moved so hypnotizing that the club-goers turned and started shouting encouraging words at her. The men on the floor stood in front of their section matching her movements, hoping to be invited in. Mikayla sat back enjoying the show until her cousin reached back and pulled her up to where she was.

"Close your eyes and feel the music."

Mikayla started to sway to the music matching Alba's rhythm. Angel walked back to their section and held her arms to be patted down by Mateo. Once permitted to enter, she walked in at placed the drinks on their table. She caught Mikayla's attention again when she bent over. As soon as she returned to an upright position, Mikayla grabbed her hand. "Dance with us!"

The music switched to an Afro Caribbean song, and the crowd went wild. Alba pointed at two guys in the crowd and waved them to her. When they got close enough, she told them to come in. They walked around to the entrance of their section where they were stopped by Mateo who told them to go back. Alba whined.

"Please Mateo, you're right there. We just want to have fun."

Against his better judgment, he started to pat the men down. He removed a gun from each one of their waistbands. The guns put him on high alert, but Alba stepped forward and pulled them inside before he could protest. Another salsa song came on, and Alba was pulled into a spin by the cutest one. His less attractive friend sat on the couch and motioned for Mikayla to come towards him. She ignored him and instead grabbed Angel and started to dance with her. The man yelled something out in Spanish causing Angel to abruptly stop dancing. She pulled away from Mikayla and made her way to the rope that Mateo opened. He was now facing them. Mikayla sighed and reluctantly went to the couch and put a little bit of distance between herself and the less attractive friend.

"I'm Manolito," he screamed out over the music. His accent was thick, but his English was perfect.

Mikayla rolled her eyes slightly. "Mikayla."

"Nice to meet you. You're American?"

Mikayla looked at him with a scowl on her face. "I guess so."

"Are you a Sanchez?"

Mikayla's ears perked up. She was very street smart and had seen Mateo remove their guns. They had to be people of importance to get past the metal detectors with their guns still on them. She instead countered his question with one of her own.

"The better question is, who are you?" Manolito took a sip of his drink. He glanced in the direction of Alba before he answered.

"Manolito Flores."

Mikayla's ears instantly started to burn. Her grandmother had spoken of a rival family. Camila's family was the Flores family. Mikayla glanced at Alba and then at Mateo who was busy at the moment patting Angel down again. Angel entered and placed a bottle of Don Q rum on the table in front of them. Manolito smiled at her with the sleaziest grin. "Mikayla, do you like rum?"

"I prefer cognac."

Manolito laughed. "That's because you've never had this rum."

He opened the bottle, grabbed a glass, and filled it halfway. Mikayla grabbed the glass from his hand and smelled it. Alba turned around and came over, grabbing a glass for herself.

"This is my favorite rum."

Everyone poured themselves a glass, and Alba proposed a toast.

"To the Sanchez family and my beautiful cousin from America!"

Mikayla watched the men exchange knowing glances and clinked glasses with them all.

"Salud!"

Mikayla took a sip of her drink and was pleasantly surprised at how smooth the rum was. She watched as Manolito took the bottle and attempted to refill everyone's glass. She stood and walked towards Mateo. "I need to go to the restroom."

Mateo pulled out his walkie talkie and called for two bouncers. When the bouncers showed up, he told them to watch the section until he came back. Mikayla called for Alba, advising they were going to the restroom. She waved at her suitor and blew him a kiss.

"I'll be right back. They exited VIP and followed Mateo through the crowd as he led them to the restroom. Mikayla looked towards their section and saw the Flores men looking in their direction. Mateo entered the ladies' restroom and told everyone to get out. The women shrieked and rushed out of the restroom. He immediately locked the door behind them. Mikayla bit her lip nervously.

"The men in our section are from the Flores family."

Mateo's smile left his face. "How do you know that?

Mikayla looked at Alba, ignoring her shocked expression. "The one sitting by me talks too much. He figured I was American and didn't know any better."

Alba stomped her foot and pouted. "We can never just have fun!"

Mateo took his cell phone out and made a call. Meanwhile, he watched Alba as she walked into a stall and locked the door behind her. Mikayla didn't know what she was saying but could tell she was pissed as she yelled at Mateo in Spanish. Once she came out and washed her hands, Mateo removed his gun and took the safety off.

"When we leave out of here, we head straight to the exit!"

Mikayla stood at the door. "They were watching us."

Mateo nodded. "I just created a distraction." On cue, officers stormed the club and caused a commotion that would allow them to slip out undetected. Mateo unlocked the door and walked along the sides of the wall farthest away from VIP. They walked out into the night air where another bouncer handed Mateo the keys and he opened the door to let the women inside their vehicle. He started the ignition and turned the truck around. When pulled into the street, traffic stopped. Something willed Mikayla to turn around, and she saw the two Flores men run into the street with their guns drawn as Mateo sped away.

25
Left Me on Read

Karina walked up behind Kenya and embraced her in a hug. "I've missed you so much!"

Kenya leaned back in her chair and squeezed her hand.

"Not as much as I've missed you. Let me stand so I can give you a proper hug."

They stood in the middle of the lobby rocking and swaying. "I haven't meant to stay away for so long. It's just been so different."

They broke the embrace and Karina stepped back. "I understand, baby. Life continues no matter what happens. You're a wife and a mom too now. When you're an entrepreneur, you are focused on making sure your baby is well-fed. Speaking of babies. What did you have?"

Kenya grabbed her phone from her purse and pulled up pictures of Dre. Karina gasped.

"Oh, my goodness! He looks just like Shannon. Ooh, I miss him so much."

Kenya leaned towards the desk and handed Karina a tissue. "I know. We all do."

She dabbed at her eyes and embraced Kenya again. "You have made my day. What can I do for you today?"

Kenya motioned at Kim. "It's been so long since we hung out, so I decided to make it a girls' day. This is my niece Kimberly. We're going to have full service."

Karina turned to face Kim. "Hello, pretty girl. I'm Karina."

Kim smiled and waved shyly. "Hi."

Karina turned back to Kenya. "We'll start with pedicures and move on from there. Two glasses of bubbly coming up."

She winked at Kenya. Kim's ears perked up. "She's going to give me alcohol?"

Kenya laughed. "It's called sparkling cider. No alcohol."

Kim pouted. "Aww, man."

Karina waved to join her in the pedicure area. She handed each one a champagne flute once their feet were in the water. Kim took her phone out and snapped a picture of her drinking from her flute. Kenya watched her edit the picture and post it to her social media.

"I hope you put that it was no alcohol."

Kim laughed. "I'm twelve, auntie! My friends know I don't drink alcohol."

Kenya leaned over to her niece's chair. "Let's take a selfie."

Kim held the camera up and snapped a picture. "Ooh, we are cute! I'm posting this one, too!"

Kenya laughed. "I just want to stop time. I don't want my baby to grow up."

Kim laughed. "I'll always be your baby. I wish I could say the same about Auntie Kai."

Kenya gasped. "Have you talked to her? Why'd you say that?"

Kim put her phone back in her bag. "The last couple of times that I called her she didn't answer the phone.

When she finally did answer the phone, she seemed like she was irritated."

Kenya's pressure rose. "Did she say something mean to you?"

Kim bit her lip nervously. "Kind of. She said, 'Why do you keep calling me? I'm busy!'"

Kim's eyes teared up and that instantly set Kenya on fire. She continued, "I said I just miss you and wanted to hear your voice."

She got extremely quiet and sniffled. Kenya didn't press her. She simply waited for her to start back talking on her own. Their attendants approached and patted for them to take their feet out of the water.

"So, she was like, well you don't have to keep calling me. If I don't answer that means I'm busy, and then she hung up the phone."

Kenya ran her fingers through her hair. "Have you called her since?"

Kim shook her head no. "I did text her and tell her I loved her."

Kenya massaged her temples. "Did she respond?"

Kim shook her head no. "She just left me on read."

"Did you tell your parents about this?"

"No, because I've already heard my dad yelling at her on the phone about not coming to see granny."

Kenya shook her head. "It's a lot going on with your aunt right now. Sometimes people go through things and take it out on the people they love the most."

Kim laid her head back on the chair. "I don't know. I wrote her a letter telling her how I feel about her, and I guess I'll give it to her whenever I see her."

Kenya looked at Kim with sympathy in her eyes. She didn't really know what was going on with Kai, but it was definitely deeper than surface value. She did know that she wasn't ready to give up on her wife just yet.

26
Mind Your Manners

Kenya walked into the waiting room of the hospital carrying a drink holder containing several cups of coffee. Dre walked beside her sipping his strawberry cream drink, unsure of their reason for being here. Kaleb looked up, smiled, and stood up to help her. He took the coffee and leaned over to kiss her on the cheek.

"Thank you, sis."

Kenya smiled at Amber and walked over to Doris to hand her a coffee. "Hey, mama. How are you feeling?"

Doris looked up at her with the saddest eyes. You could see the worry all over her face. "Hey, baby. I'm okay. Just waiting to hear something. No one has come to tell us anything."

Dre interrupted Doris saying anything else when he climbed into her lap and laid his head on her shoulder. She smiled and kissed the top of his head.

"Hey, my big boy. I've missed you so much."

Amber moved so Kenya could sit between her and Kaleb. "I started to text you and tell you to drop him off at the house, but it looks like he was the perfect distraction."

Kenya glanced at Dre and his grandmother laughing while he explained who the characters on his shoes were.

"What happened?"

Kaleb leaned into her and spoke in a whisper. "We went over to help get him out the bed so they could start their day, and he was unresponsive. Almost cold to the touch..."

"Oh, my goodness. Has anyone said anything to you yet?"

Kaleb wiped at his tears. "Just that he had hemorrhages on his brain and had to go into emergency surgery."

Amber touched her arm and whispered. "Did you get in touch with Kai?"

Kenya shook her head no. "Her phone just keeps going to voicemail. I'll try again."

Kaleb frowned. "I don't understand what's going on with my sister. Why does it feel like she's pushing everyone away? Has everything been okay at home?"

Kenya paused wondering if she should mention that Kai had not stayed at home for the last two months. "A lot is going on with Kai right now that I don't understand. When's the last time that you spoke with her Kaleb?"

He rubbed his hand over his beard. "I haven't. Every time I call it goes straight to voicemail. I feel like I haven't talked to her since the beginning of the year, and now she's not showing up for our fucking dad!"

Kaleb's raising his voice caused Doris to look over at him. "Kaleb! Mind your manners."

He shrunk into his seat and looked like he was eight years old at that moment.

"I'm sorry, momma."

Dre climbed off Doris's lap and walked over to his mom. "I have to use the restroom."

Kenya stood and sat her coffee in the seat behind her. "We'll be right back."

Before she could walk out of the door, Doris called her name. "Kenya, is Kai on her way?"

Kenya looked at Kaleb who shook his head to encourage her to lie. "Yes ma'am, she should be. I left her a voicemail."

Before Doris could say anything else the doctor walked into the waiting room. "Johnson family?"

Everyone stood and rallied around Doris. Kaleb stepped forward. "Yes. We're the Johnson Family."

The doctor looked at them with a blank expression. Kenya stared into his face looking for a clue in his eyes. "We were able to stop the hemorrhaging, but as we were closing him back up his pressure dropped."

Kaleb sat beside his mother and placed his arm around her shoulder. "So, is he okay? When can we see him?"

The doctor took his surgical hat off and wrung it in his hands. "I'm so sorry. We lost him."

27

I Forgive You

Alba embraced Mikayla in a hug as she pouted. "You're my favorite cousin in the whole world! I wish you would just stay."

Mikayla reached out and rubbed Alba's long brown hair out of her face and tucked it behind her ear. "I have some things I need to do first, but I'll miss you like crazy."

Alba stood from her bed and grabbed her phone. "Let's take a selfie. I'll send it to you, and hopefully, it will make you come back sooner. I have never had as much fun as I had with you. You make Papa let his guards down some."

Mikayla laughed. "Uncle Javi is just protecting his only child. He knows how scary the world is."

Alba held the camera out in front of them and snapped. She pulled it back and looked at it. "We are such a good-looking family. She showed it to Mikayla who nodded in agreement.

"What's your phone number?"
"555-678-9872"

Alba punched the number into her phone and looked at Mikayla. "You use Micah's phone?"

Mikayla hesitantly shook her head yes. "You talked to Micah, too?"

Alba laughed. "I talked to Micah all the time. He was more like a big brother though."

A knock on the door stopped them from continuing their conversation. Alba walked to the door and cracked it open. Mateo stood at the door and looked in at Mikayla.

"It's time to go, Señorita."

Mikayla embraced her cousin in another hug. "I'll see you soon."

Then, she followed Mateo to the door. She stopped to hug her little cousins on the way out the front door. She followed Mateo to the truck and opened the door to get in while he put her bags in the back. He walked to her door and shook his head with a smile on his face.

"So independent like your mother."

He started the truck and drove up to the guard gate and waited. He looked in the rear-view mirror at Mikayla who'd turned all the way around, taking one last look at her family's estate.

"My flight doesn't leave for four hours. Can we make a pit stop?"

~

Mikayla stood up and stretched. She'd been sitting at Evelyn and her father's grave for the last hour. Since today was her last day in Puerto Rico, she felt this was the perfect time to visit her father. She hadn't known that his body had been sent back to Puerto Rico until the day of Evelyn's burial. It had caught her by surprise to read the name on the headstone next to Evelyn's plot. She talked to them both about her life and the things that she'd been through growing up. She filled them in on the story her mother had told them about that side of the family and why she'd never tried to find them before.

She glanced up at Mateo standing at the truck about fifty feet away. She could feel his eyes on her behind his dark shades. She turned her back to him and continued to speak to her father.

"I forgive you, Papa. I know how hard it is to back out of a commitment you've made. It made me feel so much better to know that you were in love with mommy. I love you."

She looked over at Evelyn and smiled. "I'm so glad that I got to meet you. This has been the best week of my life. I thought I was alone in this world, but I have a whole family! Thank you for asking Javi to reach out to Micah."

She laughed and looked up at the sky. "Micah, take care of them! I forgive you for not telling me. I love you all."

Mikayla turned and walked back towards the truck. She waited for Mateo to open the back door and smiled when he closed it behind her. *I really am going to miss being treated like royalty.* Mateo did a walk around of the SUV before climbing into the driver's seat.

"To the airport, we go, Señorita!"

Mikayla bit her lip. "I wish that I could have said goodbye to Javi."

Mateo glanced at her in the mirror. "Javier is a very busy man, but he sends all of his love."

She glanced out the window, marveling at the beautiful blue ocean surrounding them.

"Mateo, thank you for everything that you've done for me this past week. I've had a guard before, but they weren't anything like you."

He laughed, understanding what she meant.

"I protect the Sanchez family. You are family. Thank you for not telling Javi that I let the Flores family into VIP."

Mikayla nodded her head. "Don't mention it. I can tell that Alba has you wrapped around her perfectly manicured finger."

Mateo smiled. "I've been her primary guard since she was born. She's like a daughter to me. You are a very smart lady. I hate that you have to go back. Javi needs someone with intelligence to turn the family business over to. As you can see, Alba doesn't make the best decisions."

Mikayla smiled. "She's smart. She's just young and wants to have fun. What exactly is the family business though?"

Mateo cleared his throat. The energy in the truck shifted and became extremely heavy. She could almost taste his nervousness.

"Mateo, I thought that we at least had a small amount of trust between us now."

He pulled up to the passenger drop-off section of the airport. "I don't want to cause any trouble Señorita."

Mikayla played with her nails and smirked. "I don't want to cause trouble for you either. I've considered going back to America and tying up some loose ends to come back. I just wondered what exactly I'd be getting myself into if I came back."

Mateo contemplated revealing the family's source of wealth. Something about the innocence on her face told him he could trust her.

"The Sanchez family is the head of the cocaine industry and has been for the last forty years."

Mikayla laid her head back, satisfied with the answer. She'd already figured as much but felt better with his confirmation. "A family of hustlers. It's in my blood."

Mateo laughed. "As I said earlier, you're a very smart woman. I do hope you come back."

He stepped out of the truck and opened Mikayla's door. "I'll stay with you until you leave."

28
Completely Off Guard

Nicole walked out of her office door and walked in Kenya's direction. "Kenya nice to see you again."

Kenya stood and held her hand out, accepting Nicole's handshake. She admired her black pantsuit and 3-inch stilettos that elongated her legs and made her look taller than she actually was.

"Do you have court today?"

Nicole laughed. "No. Not that I know of... I just feel like if you stay ready, you don't have to get ready. Follow me. We can talk in my office."

Kenya grabbed her purse and followed Nicole. Her office was as well put together as she was. Kenya admired the subtle, clean colors of her office.

"Did you remodel? I don't remember your office looking like this a couple of months ago."

Nicole smiled. "Very observant. We used my partner's office because my office was being done. She winked and flashed her million-dollar smile.

"I like a little spunk. Now, I know you didn't come down to talk décor. How can I help you?"

Kenya sat in the chair opposite Nicole. "I guess I just want a consultation."

Nicole's eyebrow raised. "Are we going back to court for Dre?"

Kenya bit her lip nervously and fidgeted in her chair. "No. I want information on how to start the process of divorce."

Nicole leaned back in her chair. "Oh. Well, there are a lot of factors. Did you sign a prenup?"

Kenya shook her head no. "We didn't. We thought we'd be in love forever. Crazy."

Nicole wrote something on her notepad. "Would you want full custody of Shannon?"

Kenya looked away and frowned. "Yes. I don't want her to have custody at all, but I don't think she'd fight for it either."

Nicole looked up at her shockingly but quickly regained her composure. "Was there infidelity?"

Kenya tapped her heels on the carpeted floor as her leg shook nervously. "Yes. I mean no. Well, there are signs that she's cheating, but I don't have proof."

Nicole scratched her head with her pen. "It would be easier to know for certain. I can use the same P.I. that I used on Lena. Lena was on her best behavior because she knew that a case was pending, but we would catch Kai completely off guard. Are you okay with that?"

Kenya nodded her head. "I'm fine with knowing the truth. How long do we have to be separated before I can file?"

"In the state of Louisiana, a year of separation is required to finalize the divorce, but you can file at any time."

Kenya twirled her fingers in her hair. "She hasn't stayed at the house for almost three months." Nicole stopped writing and looked at her. "Have you been served with divorce papers?"

Kenya shook her head no again. "She just left and never came back."

"I just have to ask. Have you been unfaithful in the marriage?"

Kenya paused and held her head down. The tapping of Nicole's pen was extremely loud in her head. Nicole's brow furrowed. "As your attorney, I will make sure that this goes as smoothly as possible, but you have to promise to be honest. Have you cheated?"

Kenya exhaled sharply. "I've recently talked on the phone with someone, but I haven't slept with them."

Nicole laughed. "Oh, that's perfectly fine. It's human nature to want comfort during difficult times."

Kenya breathed a sigh of relief. Something about the way Nicole said it made her feel like she wasn't as bad of a person as she'd been thinking. Since she'd stood Taylor up for her anniversary dinner, she avoided her at all costs.

"Drugs are involved."

Nicole looked into Kenya's eyes. "You or her?"

Kenya frowned. "Definitely her. I don't know if she's using them or selling them, but I know that she had them in the house with my child."

Nicole stopped writing. "Off the record, as a friend... I'm sorry to hear that; I loved you two together."

Kenya nodded her head. "Yeah me, too."

Nicole stood. "I'll need to see a financial report to assess your joint assets."

Kenya bit her lip. "I don't want anything from her; not even child support."

Nicole looked at her in shock. "Are you sure? Didn't she just open a second studio?"

Kenya stood. "I just want this to be done."

29
Keep It Between Us

Kenya packed Dre's suitcase with tears in her eyes. Tomorrow would be the first weekend that he would spend time with Lena. She looked over at him reading his book and smiled.

"Dre, I love you to the moon and back."

He placed his book on the floor beside his bean bag. Then, he stood up and walked towards her. "I love you too, mommy. What's wrong?"

Kenya sat on his bed and pulled him into her lap. "Do you remember that I told you that you would be going to spend time with your father's family?"

Dre nodded his head. Kenya inhaled and smiled. "I'm just going to miss you. That's all."

Dre laid his head on her chest. He was excited to meet his dad's family but didn't want to make his mom any sadder by showing it. "I leave Friday and come back Saturday?"

Kenya rubbed her hands through his hair. "No, you come back Sunday."

Dre counted his fingers. "Friday…Saturday…Sunday. That's only three days. Less than a week."

Kenya looked at him impressed. "How many days are in a week?"

Dre looked up at her and smiled when he held up his fingers. "Seven!"

Kenya said a quick thank you for her blessings. At least he was old enough to communicate. "Dre, what's my phone number and your address?"

He recited their address and both of his mom's phone number. Kenya was taken aback.

"I didn't know you knew your Maddy's phone number. Do you ever call her?"

Dre laughed. "Yes. I called her yesterday when you were in the shower."

Kenya's heart started to beat fast. "Did you talk to her? What did she say?"

Dre closed his eyes. "She said that she missed me and loved me."

Kenya pulled her phone out of her pocket and checked her call history. The last call to Kai was the day her father passed. "Dre, how did you call her?"

Dre shrugged his shoulders. "I don't know. I was talking to my pawpaw, and he gave her the phone."

"When did you talk to Pawpaw? Yesterday?"

"Yes ma'am."

"What did he say?"

"He said that he loved me too. He told me that he would miss me, and I asked him if I could come over his house. He told me I could come to his house anytime I wanted to."

Kenya's tear rolled down her cheek. She quickly wiped it away before Dre realized she was crying again. "What else did he say?"

"He said that Shannon told him to tell me hi, and then he put Maddy on the phone."

Kenya turned Dre around so that he was facing her. "Dre who is Shannon?"

Dre giggled thinking his mom was playing a game. He pointed at himself. "Me!"

Kenya took a deep breath. "No... Who is the Shannon that your pawpaw told you said hello?"

Dre suddenly looked very serious. "Oh. My dad. Big Shannon."

Kenya pulled him close to her and hugged him tightly. "Did your Maddy tell you where she was?"

Dre sighed. "I kept asking her, but she kept saying that she wasn't ready yet. She told me not to give up on her."

Kenya's hair stood up on the back of her neck. "Dre don't tell anyone else about this. Okay? We will keep this between us."

"Okay, Mommy. It's our secret."

30
Why Are You Here?

Kaleb watched Kai pull into their mother's driveway and sit there. He stood at the front door waiting to see if she was going to get out of the car. Doris had called her yesterday. It surprised everyone when Kai answered the phone. Doris asked her to show up for her father's funeral tomorrow, and she promised she would. Kaleb was shocked that she'd actually shown up since she hadn't returned anyone else's calls prior. He hoped that she wasn't trying to convince herself to leave. As if on cue, the family car pulled up, blocking her in the driveway. Kaleb opened the door and walked outside.

"Good morning."

Kai put her shades on and opened the car door. She stepped out of the car and squirmed from Kaleb's intense stare. "Where you been, Sis?!"

Kai leaned back against the hood of her truck.

"Busy. You know I opened a second studio."

"For six fucking months, Kai? When's the last time you even talked to momma before yesterday?"

Doris, Kenya, and Amber walked out the door, saving Kai from answering. Doris embraced her in a hug.

"I'm so glad you could make it, baby. I know this is hard for everybody. Thank you for coming."

Kaleb was about to protest his mom coddling Kai but halted when Amber squeezed his arm. She looked at him with pleading eyes.

"Not in front of mom."

The driver of the family car walked around and opened the door. "It's time to get a move on folks."

Kaleb and Amber both linked arms with Doris and walked her to the car. Kai walked slowly behind them staring at the ground, and Kenya walked beside her. Kenya felt relieved seeing her face, even if she was being standoffish. Her nerves had been on edge since her conversation with Dre. She was glad to see that her wife was alive and in one piece.

"Good morning, Kai."

Kai looked at her and rolled her eyes. "Why are you here? I'm so tired of seeing your face."

Kenya paused briefly but quickly regained her confidence. "I'm not going to entertain you this morning. Today's not the day for that. I loved your dad before I even knew you existed."

The question had actually caught Kenya off guard. She walked ahead of Kai and climbed in the car beside Amber before she got emotional. Kai positioned herself in the car so that she wouldn't have to look at Kenya or Kaleb but could feel their eyes burning a hole in the side of her face. Doris grabbed and squeezed her hand.

"You know, baby, your father always loved to hear you sing 'His Eye Is on the Sparrow.' You should sing it today."

Kai's hands instantly started to sweat, and she pulled them away. Barely above a whisper, she said, "I can't, Mommy."

Kaleb bit his tongue and looked out the window. Doris patted the top of Kai's hand. "I understand, baby."

They pulled up to the doors of the church, and Kai looked around in amazement at all the people and cars in attendance. Kaleb saw her expression and rolled his eyes.

"Can't believe all these people could love a family that you don't even care about, huh?"

Doris immediately scolded him. "Kaleb! Not today! Not...today!"

Amber reached across him and opened the door. "Get out, baby. Sorry, mama."

Doris dug in her pocket and retrieved a tissue. She removed her glasses and wiped around her eyes.

"Lord, be with my family."

Kai reached over and embraced her in a hug. "I'm sorry that I haven't been around, mama. I'm here now."

Doris kissed her cheek. "It's okay, baby. Everyone grieves in different ways."

Kai opened the door and climbed out of the car before grabbing her mother's hand. She waited until Doris climbed out of the car and then wrapped her arm around her.

"Put your weight on me, mama. I got you."

Kenya got out of the car feeling invisible and walked up to Amber and Kaleb. They walked up to Doris and Kai determined to look united even if they didn't feel it. Kaleb grabbed Doris's other hand and helped get her into the church. Amber glanced at Kenya and nudged her with her shoulder.

"Are you okay, Sis? The vibe is weird between y'all."

Kenya nodded her head. Today wasn't about her, and she wouldn't make it be. They walked into the church with their heads held high and gave half-smiles to the people standing. They walked to the front pew and took a seat. The funeral director gave everyone else the okay to sit down. Doris leaned over and tapped Kenya.

"Why don't you sit down here by Kai?"

Kenya shook her head but got up and sat beside Kai anyway. Kai watched her with contempt all over her face. She leaned over and whispered. "Again, why are you here?"

Kenya ignored her and focused on the choir singing. She was already hurting and couldn't focus on how Kai was treating her. The pallbearers opened the casket for one final viewing and allowed people to engage with the family. Dawn and Ryan walked up, viewed the reverend's body, and turned around to the family. They went down the line offering their condolences and hugs. Dawn reached out to hug Kai and was stopped when Kai put her arm out to keep her from coming closer. In shock, Dawn moved down to Kenya. Kenya stood and embraced her in a hug and whispered in her ear.

"I wish I was sitting by y'all."

Dawn squeezed her hand knowingly and moved forward to keep the line moving.

~

Amber opened the door to let another food carrying woman inside. The house was full of people, and they very quickly realized they'd made a mistake having the repast there. Doris sat in the living room with Kai cuddled up beside her. Kenya stood in the kitchen with Kai in her direct line of sight. She tried to leave as soon as the burial was over, but Doris had held onto her hand and said, "Y'all have to fix this, baby. Life is too short."

She walked into the living room and walked up to Kai. "Can we talk?"

Kai's face screwed up until she realized her mom was watching her. "Yeah."

She stood and walked ahead of Kenya out of the front door. Kenya followed her to her truck. Kai turned and faced her, looking annoyed.

"What's up?"

Kenya shifted her weight. "Kai, what's wrong with you? Why do you hate me so much?"

Kai ran her hand over her hair. "You exist."

Kenya stepped back, holding back her tears. "Okay, Kai. That's it. I'm not being your punching bag anymore. You don't ever have to worry about me again. You're acting just like your punk ass brother, and I'm not talking about Kaleb. Fuck you."

Before Kenya could turn on her heels Kai smacked her. "Say it again, bitch!"

Kenya stumbled from the impact but immediately lunged at her. "Don't you ever put your fucking hands on me again!"

Amber who'd seen the exchange from the window ran from the house. "Stop! What is going on with y'all?"

Kenya stopped hitting and stepped back, wiping the blood from her lip. "Ask your stupid ass sister! Fuck this. I'm out of here."

Kenya quickly walked to her car. Amber looked at Kai like she'd lost her mind. "What is wrong with you? Why'd you hit her?"

Kai rolled her eyes and opened her car door. "Mind your own business! Go tell whoever the fuck is blocking me in to let me out this bitch!"

Amber turned and walked back to the house in shock from the way Kai talked to her. She walked up to Kaleb and asked him to come outside with her.

"Kai needs help. Something's wrong with her."

He stopped what he was doing and rushed to the door. "What's wrong with her? Where is she?"

They made it to her truck just in time to see Kai snort a bump of cocaine.

31
It's 5 'clock Somewhere

Kenya pulled up to drop Dre off in the designated area in front of the school. "What kind of day are we having?"

Dre looked at his mother's face and focused on her lip. He leaned forward and wrapped his arms around her. "I love you, mommy."

Kenya placed a kiss on his forehead. "I love you too, baby. Have an amazing day. Okay?"

The parking monitor opened the door and ushered Dre from the car. "Good morning!"

He stepped from the car and glanced back at his mother once more before walking behind the other children into the school. As soon as he walked to his homeroom door, he heard someone call his name. He turned in the direction of the man who was walking towards him.

"Hey, I'm so glad I caught you before you went in. Did your mom send you an overnight bag?"

Dre hesitated to speak to the man he'd never seen before. The man picked up that he was reluctant to talk to him. "I guess it slipped your mom's mind. She was supposed to drop you off at Grandma Lena's, but she brought you to school."

A smile crept onto Dre's face. "I'm going over to Grandma Lena's today?"

The man smiled. "Yes. We are all going to the water park. Your mom said it was okay and that she would send you some clothes for you to spend the night."

Dre looked around him. "Where is Grandma Lena?"

"She's at home packing up snacks so we can have a picnic. I'm your uncle Troy. Your dad Shannon's brother. I live over this way, and I told Grandma that I would get you."

Dre looked at his classroom door. "I haven't eaten breakfast yet."

Troy glanced at all the children starting to retreat into their classrooms and knew it was now or never. He looked at the exit door behind him. "No problem. Go ahead and go to class. I'll just tell grandma you didn't want to go. Maybe next time. I'll just tell her to put the ice cream in the freezer."

Dre's eyes widened. "Grandma Lena is going to let me eat ice cream for breakfast?"

Troy walked to the exit door. "She was, but don't worry about it, buddy. Next time."

Dre walked in his direction. "I want to go."

Troy stopped at the door and held his arms out. "Well come on."

~

Kenya waited at the door for Dawn to open it. As soon as she opened the door, her attitude went to a level ten. "What the hell happened to your face?"

Kenya walked into the house and headed straight to the couch. "Kai hit me."

Dawn walked behind her and sat beside her. "So, she abandoned Dre but now wants to be your parent? Where is she?"

Kenya shrugged her shoulders. "I don't know, and I don't care."

Dawn stood up. "It's 5'clock somewhere…you want a drink?"

Kenya shook her head no. "It's 8 a.m. here."

Dawn sat back on the couch. "Why did she put her hands on you, and when did this happen?"

"Saturday at the repast."

Dawn immediately tensed up. "I knew I should have come over there. When Ryan went to work, something told me to come back."

Kenya sighed. "I'm glad that you didn't come. I didn't want to do that at her mom's house, especially on that day."

Dawn frowned. "Did you call the police?"

Kenya's phone rang, stopping her from responding. "Why is Dre's school calling me? Hello?" Kenya listened to the automated recording and ended the call. "Why is his school calling to report him absent when I just dropped him off?"

32
That's a Promise

Kenya called Lena's number again and sighed. "Now, she's forwarding me to voicemail, but that's okay. I'm almost at her house."

Dawn held on tightly to the handle on the door. "Slow down so we can make it in one piece! What exactly did his teacher say?"

Kenya slammed on her breaks as she pulled into Lena's driveway. "She said that a little girl heard him saying Grandma Lena to some man he was talking to."

They jumped from the car and ran to her front door. Kenya and Dawn stood at Lena's door beating so hard that the frame of the door shook. Lena opened the door with a scowl on her face. "Why are y'all beating on my door like the police, and why do you keep calling my phone so much, heathen?"

Kenya pushed past her and ran into the house. "Where is he? Dre, it's mommy! Come here!"

Lena stared at her like she was crazy. "Of course, you've lost him. Why the judge thought you were a good mother, I'll never understand."

Kenya turned around and started towards her. "I will kill you."

Dawn stepped in between them. "She's not worth it!"

Lena laughed manically. "So now you're threatening to do bodily harm? Just one more thing that I can add to the list of things that you do horribly."

Kenya burst into tears. "Lena, where is my child?"

Lena seemed to momentarily feel sympathy but quickly pushed it away. "No matter how pathetic I know you are, I would never steal Shannon. Who have you pissed off now?"

Kenya ignored her and called out for Dre once more. "Dre, it's mommy! Scream if you can hear me."

Lena became annoyed at this point. "You have one minute to get out of my house, or I'm calling the police. If I did take him, do you think I'd be dumb enough to bring him here?"

She opened her door. "Get the fuck out of my house! I'll make sure to let the courts know about this incident, too."

Dawn grabbed Kenya's hand. "Come on, Kenya. He's not here. We need to call the police."

Lena looked at her evilly. "You haven't even called the police yet? Oh, my goodness how dumb can you be? Maybe you should call your dyke wife and ask her if she has him."

Kenya turned and faced her. "You are the evilest woman I have ever met in my life. If you really cared about Dre the way you pretended to, you'd be just as worried. If I find out that you had anything to do with this, beating your ass will be a promise!"

Dawn took her phone out and dialed 9-1-1 as she walked to the car. "I'd like to report a missing child."

Kenya walked away from Lena and followed her friend to the car. She listened as Dawn answered the operator's questions. "The last place he was seen was at Highland Elementary. His mom dropped him off around 7 a.m. and received a call about an hour later that he was absent from school."

Kenya opened the door and climbed into the driver's seat. Dawn touched her arm and put her phone on speakerphone. "Where do you want them to meet you?"

Kenya sighed. "We're on the way to his school; they must have some type of cameras."

The operator pecked on her keyboard. "Is this Highland Elementary?"

Dawn nodded her head. "We're on the way to Highland."

Kenya pulled out of the driveway and headed towards the school.

"What is this child's full name, and how old is he?"

Dawn held her head down. "Shannon Deandre Sanchez-Johnson. He's five years old."

"What was the child wearing the last time he was seen."

Dawn waited for Kenya to answer and repeated the question when she didn't respond.

"Kenya, what did he have on this morning?"

Kenya ran her fingers through her hair. "He had on his uniform. White polo shirt, navy shorts, and white Nike sneakers."

"Did she say school uniform with white Nike sneakers?

"Yes, ma'am, that's correct."

"Did he have a backpack?"

Kenya sighed. "Yes! He has a black panther backpack. It's black and gold."

They listened as the operator punched the keys on the keyboard some more. "Okay. We already have officers at the school, and they are waiting to talk to you."

Dawn turned the speaker off. "Okay. Thank you. We will be there in two minutes."

Kenya pulled into the school parking lot so fast that she caused the officers in front of the school to look up. She slammed her car in park and jumped from the car when she saw one of the officers holding Dre's backpack.

"Did you find him?"

The officer stopped her in her tracks. "The school's on lockdown, ma'am. I'm going to need you to get back in your car."

Kenya's eyes filled with tears. "What! I'm the missing child's mother. That's his backpack that man is holding. Where did he get it from?"

The detective that was checking the contents of the backpack walked over. "Mrs. Johnson?"

Kenya nodded her head. "Did you find him?" "Our dogs found this in the parking lot, and we're still searching for a scent."

33
Bon Appetite

Kenya sat at the table replaying the last morning she'd seen Dre. She combed her memory for any signs she'd missed. It had been a week since she'd last seen her baby. She felt like she was losing her mind. They were able to see the man on the camera but could not identify who he was. He'd been smart enough to avoid the cameras. As she thought about the days leading up to Dre's disappearance, her phone rang and startled her. She checked the caller ID, and her heart began to beat fast. She gathered her strength to answer, afraid of who was on the other end of this unknown number.

"Hello."

Taylor's voice boomed from the other end.

"Hey, Ms. Kenya! Long time, no hear."

Kenya sighed. Her mood bordered irritation but joyful to have someone to talk to. Dawn had stayed with her every night, but she had to still work and go to school. That left her alone in the daytime.

"Hi, Taylor. How are you? Why'd you call me private?"

"Oh, this is my business phone. It's an unknown number to keep people from calling me back. I broke my personal phone and won't have a replacement for a couple more days. What have you been up to?"

Kenya hesitated. It was welcomed to talk to someone without them projecting pity. Everyone felt sorry for her. Even if they didn't say it, you could see it on their faces and hear it in their voices. Lena had even put her disdain for her on the back burner and brought her a home-cooked meal.

"I really haven't been doing anything. I took leave from work for about a month, so I've just been relaxing."

Taylor laughed. "Oh, is that why you stood me up - because you've been tired?"

Kenya stood in the mirror and brushed her hair out of her face. "I've just had a lot going on. I left you a voicemail and asked if I could have a raincheck."

Taylor sighed. "Aww man; I never got that. I broke my phone around that time. Since I haven't replaced it, yet I didn't get it."

Kenya walked into her bedroom. "I'm free tonight. Do you feel like having any company?"

She could hear Taylor's smile through the phone. "As long as that company is you. Do you remember my address?"

Kenya pulled up the contact for 'dance class' and recited the address she had saved. Taylor confirmed that was correct. "How long before you can get here?"

Kenya grabbed her bag. "I'm walking to my car now."

Taylor laughed. "Uh oh. I finally get to spend some time with the infamous Kenya. I'm already cooking, so I guess I'll have to take a raincheck on the meal you promised me."

"Yeah, I guess so. What are you cooking?"

"Butter chicken. Do you like Punjabi food?"

Kenya started her car and waited until her phone connected to her Bluetooth. "Punjabi?"

Taylor laughed again. "Indian. My dad taught me how to make it. It's one of my favorite dishes. It's cooked with lots of garlic naan."

"I've never had It. Are you Indian?"

"Half. My dad is from Pakistan, but my mom is black"

"Oh. I figured you were biracial, but I didn't want to assume."

Kenya listened as Taylor moved around in her kitchen and laughed when she cursed out loud. "Do you want me to let you go? I don't want you to burn your food."

Taylor laughed. "Nah. I'm not burning our dinner. You just have me so distracted that I grabbed a hot pan."

Are you okay? Put some cold butter on it."

Taylor opened her freezer and grabbed a stick of butter. "Do I take the paper off?"

Kenya laughed, enjoying the moment. "Not unless you want the butter to melt in your hand. You've never heard of that. You just want something cold to absorb the heat to try to stop the skin from blistering."

Taylor smiled. "I like that. Taking care of me already. I never asked you what your profession is. Are you a doctor?"

Kenya smiled. "I'm a stylist."

"Oh, word. When can I schedule an appointment?"

Kenya laughed. "What exactly would you want me to do your hair? You have locs."

"Anything that you come up with. I guess we can see what you think when you finally get here."

"Well, you should open the door."

Taylor walked to the door and stepped back allowing Kenya inside. "Come in. Welcome to my humble abode."

Kenya ended the call and walked inside. She checked out Taylor's home. It was spotless and definitely a bachelor pad. "It smells amazing in here."

"Funny… I was just about to say the same thing to you. Let's sit at the table; I'm starving."

Kenya pulled a chair out and sat after hanging her bag on the back. Taylor fixed their plates and glanced at Kenya. "You want a glass of wine or a beer?"

"If you have red wine, I'll take that. If not, water will be fine."

Taylor smiled. "What kind of gentlewoman would I be without a good Merlot on my hands?"

Kenya nodded. "My favorite."

Taylor brought the bottle and two wine glasses and placed them on the table before returning to get the plates. She sat Kenya's plate down, pulled the chair out beside her, and took a seat. Kenya leaned down and inhaled her food.

"Wow. This is not what I expected when you said butter chicken."

Taylor smiled. "Wait until you taste it."

She caught Kenya off guard when she grabbed her hand and said grace over the food. Kenya waited for Taylor to eat before she picked up her fork. Taylor grabbed the wine and poured each of them a glass.

"Bon appétit."

Kenya watched her place a fork full of chicken into her mouth followed by a piece of the tortilla looking bread. Kenya mimicked her and was pleasantly surprised at how good the food was.

"It's not spicy at all. I thought all Indian food was spicy."

Taylor smiled and took a sip of her wine.

"When you make your own, you control the spice level."

Kenya took another bite of her bread. "This bread is so good. What's it called again?"

"This is garlic naan. I can eat this just about every day."

Kenya nodded her head in agreement and continued to eat her food. She hadn't realized that she was this hungry and hadn't eaten all day. She placed her fork on her empty plate and looked over at Taylor embarrassed. Taylor smiled and sopped the remaining sauce from her plate.

"Either I'm a really great cook or I wasn't the only one starving."

Kenya laughed. "You're a great cook. Thank you for giving me a new experience. I'll clean the kitchen up."

Taylor watched her grab the plates and take them to the kitchen. She licked her lips as she admired the way her jeans fit. Kenya caught her staring and tried to lighten the mood. "Are you sure you cooked this? Where are all the dishes?"

Taylor laughed. "I clean as I go."

She refilled both of their glasses and walked into the kitchen with Kenya. The space was small and provided the perfect opportunity to squeeze up behind her while she dried the plates off. Kenya placed the plates in the drying rack and turned to face her. Her breast pressed against Taylor's body, as she grabbed the glass from her hand and finished it off. As soon as she took the glass from her lips, Taylor leaned over and kissed her. She half expected Kenya to push her off but was pleasantly surprised when she kissed her back. She sat her glass down and picked Kenya up. Kenya wrapped her legs around her waist as Taylor turned and carried her out of the kitchen into her bedroom.

Still passionately kissing her, she laid Kenya on her back and started to lift her shirt. She slowly began biting her nipples through her lace bra. She simultaneously reached down and unbuttoned Kenya's jeans and then slid her hand between her legs. Kenya's moan encouraged her to keep going, so she places kisses down her stomach. Kenya's phone sounded and broke the trance she was in.

"Taylor, let me up."

She ignored her and started to slide her jeans down.

"Taylor, let me up!"

Taylor backed off her and watched Kenya run to the front for her phone while putting her clothes back on in the process. Kenya grabbed her phone and checked the alert. Kai had just entered the code to their alarm system. She checked the cameras and saw Kai going into her office with a stack full of papers. She grabbed her purse. "Taylor, I'm so sorry. An emergency just came up. I'll call you later."

34

It All Makes Sense

Kenya pulled into the yard beside Dawn's car. Kai's truck was nowhere in sight. She went through the garage door, startling Dawn.

"Girl, I know this is your house, but you better announce yourself!"

She looked at Kenya curiously. "Why are you looking so flushed? Where have you been?"

Kenya ignored her and walked towards Kai's office. "How long have you been here."

"About five minutes. Why what's up?"

Kenya opened the office door with Dawn right on her heels. "Was Kai here when you came?"

Dawn shook her head no. "Nobody was here. Why am I the only one answering questions?"

Kenya sighed. "My alarm system alerted me that Kai used her code to get it, but I never saw her leave."

She glanced at her phone and saw that it was still showing the lights on in the house, but she and Dawn were not on the screen even though she was directly in front of the camera.

"What the hell? She paused the camera?"

Kenya started the camera back and immediately saw Dawn looking at the camera.

"Kenya, what is going on?"

Kenya walked to Kai's desk and punched in her birthday to unlock the desk. There was a folder containing a stack of papers that wasn't there previously in the drawer. She took the folder out and started to inspect the contents. The folder contained invoices, receipts for rent, a rental car, and cash withdrawals.

"So, the bitch has a rent house?! Wow."
She continued to flip through the papers until a birth certificate caught her attention.

"What the hell is this?"

Dawn walked over to her and studied the birth certificate with her.

"What is Kai doing with a Puerto Rican birth certificate?"

Kenya shrugged. "I don't know. The better question is why does this list a set of triplet girls?"

Dawn read the names on the paper. "Baby-A Mikayla Sanchez, Baby-B Kai Sanchez, and Baby-C Micah Sanchez."

Kenya grabbed the chair and sat down. "What the hell is going on? They are triplets?"

She glanced up at Dawn who looked like she was about to be sick. "Dawn, what's wrong with you? Your face just went completely white. Is there something you aren't telling me?"

Dawn walked over and sat on the couch. "Have you ever seen Mikayla?"

Kenya shook her head. "I didn't even know she existed."

Dawn placed her head in her hands. "I know her. It all makes sense now. She played me."

Kenya looked at her confused. "I don't know what's going on, but this isn't real. Micah's birthday was in February not July. Micah was also an only child."

Dawn frowned. "Kenya, no he wasn't. Did you forget that he and Kai have the same dad?"

Kenya shook her head. "No, I didn't forget, but this has to be fake. We saw both Kai's and Micah's birth certificate together. They were both listed as single births, Dawn. Micah had blue eyes, remember? I don't know what Kai is doing."

Dawn looked up at the ceiling. "Kenya, that means nothing! Either the birth certificates we saw that night were fake or this one is. I need to reach out to Mikayla. She has to make sense of this. I was being too reckless and never asked her many personal questions."

Dawn took her phone out and dialed the number she had programmed for Mikayla. "The line is disconnected!"

Kenya looked at Dawn like she was losing her mind. "Dawn, who the hell is Mikayla? And why do you think it's the same person if you don't even know her? Where did you meet her?"

Dawn exhaled as she laid her phone on the cushion beside her. "At a club. In hindsight, it looks like I was targeted. I slept with her. I let her sleep with my man."

Kenya massaged her temples. "Wait. You did what?"

Dawn continued, ignoring Kenya's questions. "I invited her to my house."

Kenya's phone rang, halting her from asking any more questions. "Hello?"

Nicole closed her office door and sat at her desk. "Hey, Kenya. How are you? I second-guessed calling you because I know that you have a lot on your plate right now. I saw Dre on the television. Have the police found anything?"

Kenya sighed. "Not yet. They said after forty-eight hours, the chances of finding him alive diminishes drastically. I've been praying that Kai has him, but she won't answer my calls."

Nicole cleared her throat. "She's actually the reason I'm calling. My guy has been tailing her."

Kenya stood up abruptly, knocking the papers from the desk. "Does she have Dre?"

"No, but I do have the address of the woman she's been staying with."

Kenya grabbed a notepad. "Give it to me!"

35

It's Not Safe

Dawn stood dumbfounded as she watched Kenya put her hair in a ponytail. She was dressed in all black and looked like a scene out of a movie.

"Where are you going? Who was that on the phone?"

Kenya sat on the bed and tightened her sneakers as she avoided eye contact. "I'm going to get answers."

Dawn shifted her weight from one leg to the other one. "Answers from whom?"

Kenya ignored her and stood to her feet. She walked back to Kai's office and retrieved her purse. Her phone buzzed to alert her of a missed text. She unlocked the screen and saw the text from an unknown number. Her mind instantly went to Taylor's business line, making her frown. *Not now Taylor.* She chose not to read it. Instead, she opened her bag to place her phone inside. Before she could put her phone into the bag, it buzzed again. She hit the text thread and opened the attachment first. The scream that came from her caused Dawn to rush to her side. Kenya burst into tears and Dawn grabbed the phone from her hand.

"Oh, my goodness!"

Panic set in as she zoomed in on the picture of Kai and Dre gagged and bound to a chair.

Dawn exited the picture and read the original message aloud.

"Do not call the police if you want to see them alive. Get in your car and start driving alone. Once I make sure you aren't being followed, I'll send you an address.

Kenya grabbed her keys and ran to the front door. Dawn ran behind her, catching up to her quickly.

"Kenya who did this come from?"

Her face was covered in tears as she fumbled to unlock her car door. "I don't know, Dawn. It's an unknown number."

Dawn reached for the keys. "Let me drive."

Kenya snapped at her. "They said alone! I have to do this by myself. I can't put his…their… life in jeopardy."

Dawn panicked. "Kenya, it's not safe to go by yourself!"

Dawn was unsure of what to do next as she watched Kenya back out the driveway. She ran into the house, grabbed her cellphone, and dialed Ryan's number. She paced the floor as she waited for him to answer. He answered the phone with a smile.

"Hey, my beautiful fiancée!"

Dawn shouted on the phone. "I need you!"

The panic in her voice put him on high alert.

"Baby, what's wrong? Where are you?"

Dawn locked the house up and ran to her car. "I'm at Kenya's house, but I need you to track her car."

Ryan turned his scanner down. "Baby, how am I going to do that? Is Kenya in trouble?"

Dawn started her car and backed out of the driveway. "She has OnStar! I really need you to find her. Someone sent her a picture of Kai and Dre gagged and tied up to a chair! She left driving, and she's waiting for instructions to meet them somewhere."

Ryan jumped out of his cruiser and jogged into the station. "Come meet me at the station. I'll send a request to OnStar right now."

36
Ghost in The Dark

Kenya pulled up to the address that she'd received about twenty minutes after she left her house. She'd been driving around aimlessly waiting for another text and had almost wrecked her car when it came through. When she received the text, she realized it was the same address that Nicole had given her earlier. Kenya had been sitting in the driveway for fifteen minutes. The house was completely dark and looked vacant. Her nerves were on edge as she looked around searching for any movement in the pitch-black night. The house was the only one on the dead-end street. Her headlights bounced off the trees and played tricks on her mind. Her phone vibrated, and she gasped when she read the text: *"Turn the car off and come to the door."*

Kenya killed her ignition and grabbed her pepper spray. She removed the safety and placed her finger on the trigger. The only sound she heard were the crickets and the thumping of her heart in her ears. As soon as she made it to the door, the knob turned slowly and the door opened, exposing a slender man that smelled of cigarettes and cheap liquor.

"Come in."

Kenya walked into the cold dark house and waited for her eyes to adjust. This had to be a mistake. There's no way Kai lived here with anyone. Her eyes adjusted and strained to focus on the room lit by nothing but the moonlight peeking through the boards on the window. The only piece of furniture in this room was a broken wooden chair laying on its side. Empty liquor bottles and beer cans were scattered around the room, covering the floor. A man stepped in front of her.

"Arms out."

She held her arms out, attempting to slide the pepper spray into the sleeve of her jacket. In one swift movement, he snatched the can and proceeded to pat her down.

"Where's your phone?"
Kenya's voice failed her and cracked. "I...I left it in the car."

Satisfied with that answer, the man placed the pepper spray in his pocket and walked towards the front door.

"Wait here. Do not move."

Kenya turned to face him and sprung for the door when he pulled it closed. A voice came out of the darkness, stopping her in her tracks.

"Didn't he tell you not to move!"

She turned in the direction of the voice but saw nothing but shadows bouncing off the walls.

"Who are you? Where are my wife and child?"

The voice seemed to move to the other side of the room.

"Come on, Kenya. You're a smart lady. Nothing about me sounds familiar?"

Kenya's heart was now in her throat. She had to be losing her mind.

"Micah?"

A slow clap erupted in the dead silence. The house being empty amplified the sound.

"I used to be, but who am I now, Kenya?"

Kenya's head started to pound. "Kai?"

The flicker from a lighter pulled her attention to the corner of the room. The flame illuminated her face when she lit the end of her cigar, and Kenya shrieked.

"Kai, what is going on? What kind of sick game are you playing? Where is Dre?"

She started in her direction but stopped when the infrared laser hit her face. "Don't take another step."

She quickly wiped the tears from her eyes when Kai stood up and walked towards her.

"Turn around and walk to the door at the end of the hall."

"Kai, it's pitch black in this house. I can't see the door."

Kai walked closer, placing the barrel of the gun in her back. "Walk!"

Kenya willed her legs to move and walked to the door at the end of the hall. Kai pressed the gun into her back harder. "Open the door, stupid!"

Kenya turned the knob and pushed the door open. Dre's eyes widened, and he called out to her.

"Mommy!"

Kenya ran to Dre and pulled him into her arms. She heard a loud clank when something yanked him back and pulled them both down to the mattress on the floor he'd been sitting on. Dre cried out in pain, and she realized his arm was chained to a pipe that had been bolted to the floor.

"Kai, what the hell is wrong with you? Unchain him!"

Kai laughed and removed her hair from the bun it had been held in. "Kenya, I know you aren't really this dumb."

Kenya looked around the room for a weapon but knew that Kai would shoot her before she could make it to the lamp sitting on the floor in the middle of the room. The lamp lit up the room and almost seemed too bright in contrast with the rest of the house. She stared into her face.

"Kai, please let us go. I've already started the process of divorce. I don't want anything from you. I'm begging you to please let us go."

Kai laughed the evilest laugh. "You were always too emotional for your own good. So annoying."

She glanced towards the closed bathroom door. "You heard that lil sister? It didn't take much for her to give up on you!"

Kenya looked at her in confusion. "Who are you talking to? Are you high?"

Kai laughed and kicked the bathroom door open revealing a gagged Kai sitting on the bathroom floor with her hands tied behind her.

37

Identity Crisis

Kenya looked from the person standing in front of her to the person sitting on the floor. Realization registered on her face. "You're identical? Mikayla?"

Mikayla waved her gun in the air. "It took you long enough, dummy!"

She pointed her gun at Kai. "Get out here. Let's have a family reunion."

Kai grabbed the edge of the tub and positioned herself to stand. She was dressed in the same suit Kenya had packed for her Houston trip six months ago. It was stained and ripped. Her frizzy hair was stuck to her sweaty forehead. Kenya looked into her dirty tear-stained face speaking her thoughts aloud.

"It wasn't you...the whole time she's been pretending to be you."

Kai sat on the mattress next to Dre and slid close enough to nudge him on the forehead. Dre sniffled from his tears and buried his face into Kenya's side. Dre's fears seemed to enrage Kai even more and made her yell something that no one understood because of the towel stuffed in her mouth. Mikayla laughed and pointed her gun at Kenya.

"You're like Sanchez kryptonite. I just don't understand what they see in you. Remove the towel from my sister's mouth, dumbass."

Kenya reached over and pulled the filthy towel from Kai's mouth and tossed it on the floor. "Baby I'm so sorry. 1 didn't know."

She grabbed at the fabric holding Kai's hands together and tried to release them. Mikayla's scream startled her and caused Dre to cry out in fear.

"Back off! I didn't tell you to release her hands."

Kai took a deep breath and choked as she tried to catch her breath. "Dre, look at me!"

Dre turned his head and stared into Kai's face.

Mikayla laughed. "No, Dre. Look at me."

Dre buried his face into Kenya's side again, and she wrapped her arms around him. Kai attempted to lunge at Mikayla who instantly turned the gun on her.

"Don't play hero, sis."

Kai sat back down on the mattress and shook her head in defeat. Mikayla backed up to the wall behind her and grabbed a stack of pictures off the only other piece of furniture in the room – a small wooden table. "

"Kai, I do have to apologize to you. No matter how much you actually helped me pull this off, I feel bad about hurting you. You're like the best supporting actress. Tell me something. Did you know?"

Kai looked at her in confusion. "Did I know what?"

Mikayla laid a copy of the birth certificate in her lap. "Kenya, I wish I could have seen your face when you saw it."

Kai looked at the paper and then at Kenya. "You knew this?"

Kenya shook her head. "I just found out tonight. She left a copy at the house." She looked at Mikayla. "Why? If you were going to do this, why'd you want me to see it?"

Mikayla laughed. "I just wanted to get your adrenaline rushing. I get a kick out of making you angry."

Kai looked down at the paper. "How is this possible? My birth certificate shows that I was born here in America."

Mikayla shook her head. "Fake. Turns out we come from a family of hustlers. That explains where you got your sense of business from. You've created quite the empire. I hope I didn't screw up things too bad."

Kai raised her hands rubbing her arm over her face to get the tears out of her eyes. "My mother's name was Camila."

Mikayla stumped her foot. "That was not your mother! Your mother's name was Isabel!"

Kai laid her head back on the wall. This was all too much to process.

"I guess Kaleb really isn't my brother either huh?"

Mikayla found this to be the perfect time to apply her signature red lipstick to her lips.

"Unfortunately. His bitch of a mother blackmailed our mom for you because she couldn't have another child. Our mother died of a broken heart trying to find you. I promised to let you know that she searched for you."

Mikayla glanced behind her in the filthy bathroom mirror. "Ugh. So plain. It was so hard pretending to be you, but it was fun."

Kai shook her head. "You're sick."

Mikayla clicked her tongue. "What I am sick of is this bitch targeting our family and y'all falling for it. I mean the sex is good but not that damn good."

Kenya who'd sat there in silence rocking Dre finally spoke.

"Liar. We never had sex! I only gave..."

Mikayla sucked her teeth, interrupting Kenya.

"Tsk, tsk, tsk. Yes, we did, Kenya! I'm not talking about that drunken mess in the kitchen a few weeks ago. You gave it to me for almost two years. You really could never tell when Micah and I switched places?"

Mikayla tucked her hair behind her ear. "Of course, you couldn't. I'm convinced that you're a little slow. Did we all taste the same?"

Kai frowned. "Stop speaking to my wife like that!" She turned and looked at Kenya with pity. "What the hell is she saying Kenya?"

Mikayla interrupted her before she responded.

"I'm saying your perfect little angel is a whore! She gives it up to whoever wants it. Isn't that right, Kenya?"

Mikayla tossed the remaining pictures at Kai's feet. Kenya picked up one of the pictures and stared at the image of her and Taylor from earlier this evening. She was instantly filled with regret. Her eyes filled with tears, and she searched Kai's face. "I'm so sorry, baby. I thought that you didn't love me anymore. She told me she hated us."

Kai remained composed and grabbed Kenya's hand and squeezed it. "She manipulated this whole thing. I can only imagine what she has put you through. I'm so sorry that you both had to go through this. I love you."

Mikayla lost it and aimed her gun at the ceiling, pulling the trigger. "Stop it!"

Kenya laid her body on top of Dre's, shielding him from the falling sheetrock. Kenya searched her mind for a solution. She would sacrifice her life if it meant saving Dre.

"Mikayla, it's me that you want. The only thing I ask is that you don't do it in front of him. Let them go. Please!"

Mikayla scratched her head with the barrel of the gun. "Finally! A great idea comes out of her. Get up!"

Kenya kissed Dre on the head and leaned over to embrace Kai's face. I love you both."

Mikayla pointed the gun at her. "If I tell you to get up again, your son will need therapy for the rest of his life."

Kenya stood and walked to the door and then glanced back once more at her family. Mikayla smiled at Kai. "In just a few minutes, you'll be free. I'll be right back."

She followed Kenya into the dark living room. "Any last words?"

A voice came from behind her and caught her off guard. "Drop the gun!"

Before Mikayla could turn in the direction of the voice, the front door flew open and Kenya dived to the floor. Flashlights filled the house with light as officers yelled out commands. Mikayla let the gun fall from her hand in defeat. "Fuck!"

As the officers rushed to handcuff Mikayla, Kenya jumped up screaming.

"She has my son chained up back there. I need to get my baby!"

An officer grabbed her around the waist to keep her from moving another step. "We are securing the house, ma'am. We will get him."

He dragged Kenya from the house and followed the officer walking Mikayla out in handcuffs. Kenya stepped out of the house to Dawn screaming her name. Dawn sprinted to her.

"Was he here?"

Kenya nodded her head and embraced Dawn in a hug. "Thank you for being you."

Dawn broke their connection and stepped to the side as the officer pushed Mikayla forward.

Mikayla stopped in front of Dawn and smiled.

"Hey, beautiful. I'll see you again soon."

Dawn spat at her and the officer pushed her forward. "Keep moving."

The tall slender man who'd opened the door for Kenya earlier tapped the window from inside the police car, forcing her to turn around. Tears filled his eyes as he yelled, "I'm so sorry!"

Kai emerged from the house cradling Dre in his arms, and Kenya ran towards them wrapping her arms around them. "I love you both, so much."

Epilogue

Dawn paced around the kitchen nervously, talking to herself. She turned off the fire under her grits and gave her sausage and shrimp mixture a stir.

"This is a lot of food, but it's a special occasion."

She'd been preparing breakfast for the last two hours in anticipation of Ryan coming home after his night shift. "Okay. 10:15… He should be here in just a moment. She stepped into the foyer, placing her bare feet into her heels. She glanced at herself in the mirror and rubbed her belly.

"You are my miracle baby. Are you ready to surprise daddy?" She waited for a kick or something and laughed. "I guess you're still sleepy."

She walked back to the kitchen and took a swig of her orange juice. The butterflies in her stomach caused her to laugh. "Oh, you liked that?"

She'd finally decided to schedule a doctor's appointment when she missed her period for the second month in a row. She knew that she'd gained some weight, especially when her wedding dress no longer fit. But never in her wildest dreams could she have guessed pregnancy. At the age of twenty-three, Dawn had suffered from a horrible cycle that lasted almost forty days. She'd lost a tremendous amount of blood and was diagnosed with Polycystic ovary syndrome. She'd originally been told that it would be difficult to get pregnant until a procedure revealed her left Fallopian tube as blocked. So, finally being pregnant was the best news of her life.

The timer went off on the waffle maker just as she heard Ryan's key enter the lock. *Perfect timing.* She grabbed a mug, dropped a chamomile and lavender tea bag in it, and filled it with boiling water from the kettle. She laughed when Ryan called out.

"Oooh wee, it smells good in here."

Dawn met him at the kitchen door dressed in nothing but stilettos and an apron. Ryan lost all train of thought as he checked her out from head to toe.

"Damn, I was sleepy but now I'm hungry." She smiled at him seductively and wrapped her arms around his neck. "It's just a little razzle-dazzle. How was your night?"

He cleared his throat. "Ahem. It was…long. This world is going to shit."

Dawn grabbed the mug, attempting to redirect the conversation. She couldn't allow his stressful job to ruin the mood.

"Drink this. It will help you calm down so you can go to sleep after breakfast."

He placed the stack of mail he'd grabbed on his way into the house on the table. After grabbing the mug, he palmed her ass with his free hand.

"I don't think I'm going to need this tea to wind down."

Dawn pulled away from him. "Since today is a special occasion, I wanted to do something special for you and enjoy a nice breakfast."

Ryan laughed. "Oh yeah. It is Father's Day. What did you get your daddy?"

Dawn smiled and kissed his cheek. "Which one?"

The question caught Ryan off guard, and he laughed nervously. "Do you have another daddy that I don't know about?"

She laughed and ignored his question. "I have a gift for you."

Ryan took a sip of his tea to wet his throat. "A gift for me?"

She handed him a box wrapped in light blue wrapping paper. He shook the box hoping to get some type of clue. Dawn leaned back against the breakfast nook and laughed.

"Just open it."

Ryan tore the paper off and revealed a plain white gift box. He ripped the tape off the corners of the box and pulled out a black onesie.

He looked at Dawn curiously. "A onesie?"

She winked her eye. "Turn it around and read what it says out loud."

He obliged and read: "Daddy's Partner in Crime."

He immediately stood and walked towards her and touched her stomach. "You're pregnant?"

Before she could even answer he picked her up and spun her in a circle.

"I'm going to be a daddy!"

She laughed as he placed her back on her feet. Then, she walked to the stove to retrieve his food. "Sit down. I don't want it to get cold."

Ryan sat at the table and grabbed the plates from her hands. "You need to sit down, too. I'll get whatever else you need. How many months are you?"

Dawn grabbed her robe off the coatrack and picked the mail up on her way to the seat. "Six months. There's nothing else for you to get. I've been eating the whole time I cooked."

Ryan laughed and winked. "I thought I was the one making you thick. You look so beautiful, baby. You don't even look pregnant."

Dawn laughed. "Technically, you are the one that made me thick."

Ryan laughed and stuffed a spoonful of shrimp and grits in his mouth. He stared, smiling as Dawn thumbed through the mail. Her facial expression changed and put him on alert.

"Baby, what's wrong? Are you hurting?"

She ripped open the envelope and read the contents aloud.

Dear Dawn and Ryan,

By the time you read this, a week should have passed. That means that you have exactly three weeks to get the ball rolling. s at 6:23 a.m., I gave birth to a 7 lbs. 3 oz little boy that I named Ryan. The prison that I'm in will put him in the system if no one has gotten him by one month from his birth. COME GET YOUR SON!

See you soon,

Mikayla

www.ingramcontent.com/pod-product-compliance
Lightning Source LLC
Chambersburg PA
CBHW032134170626
46808CB00006B/2231